T0154489

PRAISE FOR JAKOV LIND

"One of the most idiosyncratic writers of the twentieth century."
—*Independent* (UK)

"Jakov was a bad boy. . . . He was a coyote, a trickster. He enjoyed hash and LSD. A wicked smile played around his mouth, while witty aphorisms and deep insights tripped off his lips. He emanated inner strength—and an electric intelligence that we all wanted to emulate."
—Anthony Rudolf

"You can throw all sorts of names around in attempting to suggest the atmosphere of Jakov Lind—Kafka, Pinter, Rolf Huchhuth, Arthur Schnitzler, Sholem Aleichem, Bernard Malamud. But this won't do. Jakov Lind is an original."
—*San Francisco Chronicle*

"*Landscape in Concrete* is essentially a terrifying attempt to test possible clues which will guide man through the contemporary maze."
—*Critique*

"Jakov Lind has a splendid theatrical talent, sardonic and Pinteresque, gruff and Brechtian, with some old master, some Gogol, as his Ariadne. . . . Intricate, black, bestial."
—*New York Review of Books*

"You emerge from a Lind story as you would from a nightmare. You may try and figure out what the dream meant, and whether you can locate real-life referents in its characters, but nothing fits precisely. The meaning of the allegory slips from view."
—Sasha Weiss, *Nextbook*

SELECT WORKS BY JAKOV LIND

Soul of Wood
Ergo
Counting My Steps
Numbers: A Further Autobiography
The Trip to Jerusalem
Travels to the Enu
The Stove: Short Stories
The Inventor
Crossing: The Discovery of Two Islands .

JAKOV LIND

LANDSCAPE IN CONCRETE

TRANSLATED FROM THE GERMAN BY RALPH MANHEIM

INTRODUCTION BY JOSHUA COHEN

OPEN LETTER
LITERARY TRANSLATIONS FROM THE UNIVERSITY OF ROCHESTER

Copyright © 1963 by Jakov Lind
Translation copyright © 1966 by Ralph Manheim
Introduction copyright © 2009 by Joshua Cohen
Published by arrangement with the Estate of Jakov Lind

Originally published in German as *Landschaft in Beton*
by Luchterhand Verlag, 1963

First Open Letter edition, 2009
All rights reserved

Library of Congress Control Number: 2009900685
ISBN-13: 978-1-934824-14-6 / ISBN-10: 1-934824-14-3

Printed on acid-free paper in the United States of America.

Open Letter is the University of Rochester's nonprofit, literary translation press:
Lattimore Hall 411, Box 270082, Rochester, NY 14627

www.openletterbooks.org

For Faith

Introduction

"JAKOV LIND" WAS A PSEUDONYM for a man without a name. According to the rolls of a host of long-since defunct regimes, "Lind" was once known as Jakov Chaklan, Palestinian Jew (this was back when you could be one of those), and before that he was Jan Gerrit Overbeek, Dutch bargehand, which was the Nazi-era identity of Heinz Landwirth, Viennese. The author of *Landscape in Concrete*—and also of the stories of *Soul of Wood*, the novel *Ergo*, two other novels, another collection of stories, an Israeli travelogue, three memoirs, numerous stage and radio plays, and occasional poetry—might have been all of these people, and he might have been none. This is not meant "deconstructively," however, or in a spirit of relativism. What's being asserted here, at the beginning, is trauma. Is not knowing what to call one's self. Is not having a private name for one's self.

Landwirth was born in 1927, the year of the first trans-Atlantic telephone call, the year that television was first publicly demonstrated. Lindbergh flew to Paris; Trotsky was ousted from the Communist Party. This was not long after the collapse of the monarchy—the Austro-Hungarian Empire's dissolution, through the first of the wars, from a relatively unified official culture, German-speaking, German-writing, into a smattering of countries impoverished with insular nationalisms. The author's closest affinities lay here, with the ideal Habsburgs in their tubercular, war-wounded death throes; his childhood ailment is the Proustian languor, the mourning of a past always near, strangely distant, unlived and yet, lost: "If I'm sick I vomit broken china and golden frames," he writes in the first volume of his autobiographical trilogy. "What, if not handmade in the nineteenth century, is my Middle European soul?"

The work published under the name Jakov Lind has its deepest roots in a land—in a landscape, a *Landschaft*—that doesn't exist, in a time that had disappeared a decade before the author's birth. There's a reason that Middle Europe isn't a name featured on maps, since it can be anything, anywhere, in the mind. The Czech writer Bohumil Hrabal tells us that *Mitteleuropa* ends at the last Empire train station (which would mark that terminus in Lviv, now in Ukraine); Thomas Mann once proclaimed that Germany was wherever he was—a delusional, denying hope whose reification would have exiled the capital of the neighboring Reich, if temporarily, to Pacific Palisades, California. Lind offers a description of his impossible habitus in the second of his two German novels, *Ergo*, originally published as *Eine bessere Welt* (*A Better World*): "A town made of Liptauer cream cheese, Lipizzaner horses and Lilliputians of roast chicken, bauernschmaus, liver dumplings and liver sausage, a rhyme, a phrase, a proverb and perhaps not even that but only a waistline, a shoe size, a collar size, a hat size and perhaps not even that but only the family vault of Maria Theresa and Franz Josef and the children Kalifati, Ruebezahl, Krampus, and Nikolo Christkindl and Andreas Hofer, who died of scarlet fever, whooping cough, measles, chicken pox and Basedow's disease."

(Before we go any further, it should be said that Lind's autobiographies, written in English in London, are the only sources for information about Lind, and also about Landwirth, Overbeek, Chaklan, et al. How reliable they are depends exclusively on one's sense of humor.) His father, their father, "was a Viennese businessman without much business in the world. Half Luftmensch and half duke." A traveling salesman, Simon "claimed to be selling underwear to nuns." Patrimony lay in Galicia, far over the Tatra Mountains in Poland, which would make Landwirth *père* a true Viennese. By contrast, the portrait of the author's mother, Rosa *née* Birnbaum, is hazier; she "had no money, four children, and no help in a three-room flat." She was known as "the Saint. The Good One. The Strong One. The Patient One." The marriage was relatively happy; Landwirth was mothered by sisters—he would always be surrounded by women.

The author's war departs from this domesticity, never regained. With Hitler returning to annex his homeland, Landwirth was sent to the Netherlands on a Kindertransport, along with a sister (Ditta). His parents managed to make it to Palestine, where their ship, refused port by the British, was bombed by the Haganah. Landwirth boarded for a time at a Zionist farming school in Gouda, desultorily training for his own resettlement. When that school was shuttered amid Nazi occupation, Landwirth went underground (1943 marks the end of his formal education). Angered by the complacency of the Dutch Jews, who, he thought, were just waiting for their deportations east, Landwirth purchased appropriate papers and became Jan Overbeek; the young Dutchman explained his native German by claiming an Austrian mother, which was "true." As Overbeek, the author found work on a barge, plying the Rhine from the Hook of Holland down to the Ruhr Valley—one of the most postcard-perfect parts of the Reich. On furlough, Overbeek contracted the clap from a prostitute, and was ordered to a sanatorium to recover. There, he was recruited by a scientist-soldier to serve as a personal courier in an office attached to *Das Metallurgische Forschungsinstitut des Reichsluftfahrtministeriums*, "The Institute for Metallurgical Research of the Imperial Ministry of Air Traffic." When Allied bombs are falling even by day, and Berlin's being threatened, what's a Jew passing under false papers to do? Overbeek mimicked a Nazi. It's unconscious, Lind tells us; one nods and obeys, one adapts.

x

Overbeek had no way of knowing that this Nazi scientist, who refused to allow Overbeek any contact with friends (and certainly not with any female friends), was spying on the Reich's nuclear program, making reports on the progress of the Cyclotron to the British.

In summation: A Viennese teenager turned Dutch bargeworker turned employee of the German military machine, Overbeek was also an unwitting accomplice to espionage. "I liked Berlin. My job was hardly strenuous. I had to take some letters to certain officials in the Air Ministry on Friedrichstrasse. I delivered my letters in large brown envelopes, turned about, and said good-bye."

As "the German Empire was disintegrating faster than any empire before it," what were Overbeek's thoughts? "My mind was on girls and how to find them. How to find them first and how to find a place to take them to."

In 1945, amid *debellatio*, the author was off to the Netherlands again, then to France, hoping to make his European escape. Palestine was the idea, but thanks to another forged passport (reading Jakov Chaklan, Palestinian)—and to his manifold languages, all stamped with an accent that seemed to be Dutch—British Intelligence, then controlling the French border, refused to believe that he was a Jew. At Maubeuge, Chaklan dropped his pants— his circumcision was, apparently, convincing. He took passage to Haifa, only to find his father ill, his mother dead, his sisters miraculously grown up. A kibbutz drove him crazy, as did the religious, and so, with his name forever converted, if not his soul, he eventually, reluctantly, vagabonded his way to London. (With Lind, flux was the norm: wandering, fleeing, life lived as a sort of refugee-tourism; before settling in London, amid émigré-rich Hampstead, alongside the likes of Erich Fried and Elias Canetti, Lind crisscrossed the Continent: Vienna, Copenhagen, Paris. Occupations: in Palestine, beach photographer, fruit picker, air-traffic controller; in Europe, acting student, actor, private detective, journalist, literary and film agent, husband and father. First wife: Ida; second wife: Faith.)

London was also where the writing began—drafts initially intended, according to Lind, less for the proof that is publication than as an experiment, an interrogation accomplished on paper. Though he'd been writing fragments for years—beginning diaries then abandoning them when the poetry became too personal and the philosophy muddled in language—could Lind write fiction, could he write fiction that was truer than fact and in German, the murderers' tongue?

*

Which brings us to *Landscape in Concrete* (*Landschaft in Beton*, 1963), Lind's second published book and the novel that cemented his reputation after the freak, international success of the great, short-form *Soul of Wood. Landscape* concerns one Gauthier Bachmann of Duisburg-on-the-Rhine, an aspiring gold- and silversmith, and an oafish sergeant in the German army. The setting is Eastertide, 1944. As the book opens, Bachmann's just been released, or has escaped, from a sanitarium at Oppeln (known as Opole, in Poland), where he'd been recovering from a humiliating defeat at Voroshenko, a Soviet forest in which his entire regiment is said to have drowned in the mud—763 of them dead in the first five minutes of battle, as he tells it once, or within three hours, as he tells it another time, in October 1941.

Lind's novel narrates Bachmann's pitiful attempts to rejoin that Second Hessian Infantry Regiment, Eighth Battalion, or, failing that, to join any detachment that would have him and his formidable size (six-foot-two, three-hundred pounds; he's often described as a bear) and talents (Bachmann is in possession of the gold star for marksmanship; for "shooting twelve Russian monkeys off a roof" at Stalino, today Donetsk, in Ukraine).

Bachmann's picaresque takes him through the Ardennes (which turn out to be his ancestral region; his forebears had been Flemish), then to arctic Narvik, Norway, and finally back to Germany, to his original station in Honnef, all the while being fooled, manipulated, used, debased. As obedient and as loyal as a golem, intending only to serve, Bachmann acts as an impromptu executioner for a Norwegian madman, the former schoolteacher and current war profiteer (and double agent), Hjalmar Halftan. As Bachmann the soldier becomes Bachmann the multiple murderer, the absurd is reasserted. Criminality is only a question of context; after all, the Holocaust was legal, as are most wars. Individual hypocrisy is institutionalized as public chaos, through the total perversion of language: "Let me be a simple, normal, intelligent human being," Bachmann says. "That's plenty."

Besides the naïve, Nazi-Švejk Bachmann, and the "angekok" Halftan (who, it's noted, has the same first name as the president of the Reichsbank), essential characters include: Xaver Schnotz, a poisoner and army deserter; Peter von Göritz, a predatorily homosexual Major; the Elshoved family of Norse nobles; and Helga Okolek, Bachmann's Behemoth girlfriend, "Aryan" but with a Slavic surname. Supporting appearances are made by a lesbian gynecologist-landlady (murdered) and a Bulgarian Gypsy violinist (arrested).

As Bachmann marches east at novel's end to rejoin his regiment at the front—after it's officially ruled that he is, in fact, not insane and will not be discharged, as he'd suspected, as he'd feared—Lind's landscape is momentarily barren ("The sun hovers red and flat in the sky, unwilling either to rise or to set.") and the only thing that can be said with any certainty is that its author survived.

The book's closing section concerns an air-raid, and makes glancing mention of Rhenish barge-life, a scene of near-autobiography representative of Lind's style (and, typically, Ralph Manheim's translation is a marvel):

In the grass by the river bank [Bachmann] opened his coat
and tunic, pushed up his sweater and undid two shirt buttons. He wanted to feel his heart with his fingers. The heat
of the day lay heavy, like too much tenderness, over the
gray and green colors of the Rhine. The ticking he heard
was the engine of a barge. Then with wide-open eyes he
saw more barges floating through the mist that rose from
the water. They're carrying fuel to hell and stones for the
wall of the city of the dead. Desertion leads to a quarry.
Branches growing out of the clouds. Schnotz says: Your turn
will come. What's written on the barges? Basel, Rotterdam.
Aha! Secret names of the gates to the other world. Cement,
stones, sand. A giant is carrying them through the water
on his shoulders, wading step by step through the mud.
A fool. Who told him to do that? If he'd pick up the cargo
and throw it all overboard, and if the other giants did the
same, we'd all be saved. The chunks of red meat would be
cleared away. The crime can be discovered any day. What
then? Upstream and downstream they go, day after day like
galley slaves, they would have the power to sweep away the
danger. Only the giants are strong enough. I'm one of them.
When it is all put under the concrete and the sun shines
fiercely on it, nobody'll know any more what's underneath.
The corpus delicti will be gone. Nothing is more dangerous
than sitting still. I'm shoving off.

A word about style, then we'll shove off.

One's war became one's writing. If the Holocaust is to be
regarded as a perfection of Europe—technologically speaking,
especially—then the writing of the Holocaust might represent
a perfection of European culture: Accounts of the tragedy have
almost always been technically sterile, stylistically orderly, fac-
tual. Classical, Apollonian, to a fault. Elie Wiesel's memoirs, to

take as example the most popular, have found, within the camps, amid the gas chambers and ovens, an order to obey the logic of humanistic experience. Wiesel's sentences and paragraphs tried, and still try, to impose reason—a reason derived from a reverence of tradition, of continuity, in the face of diabolical incoherence. His works are resultantly direct, in-line, accounted-for; nowhere has Wiesel allowed evil to invade the flesh of his French prose. Hell is the subject, then, and not the object. But Lind's war was not survived in a camp. There was no *Appell* for Lind, no line-ups, no count-offs; there was no order in his survival, and so no order in his prose. His writing is disorganized, ungrammatical (Lind's German was brilliant but, in every respect, adolescent). His war was riven with evasions and impersonations, and so, too, is his fictional landscape. He is the one Jewish novelist of the Holocaust who, in a major European language, expressed the Holocaust not through language, but *in language. As language.* (One has to read in Yiddish to find anything comparable.) To be sure, this was aestheticizing horror. To be sure, this is what writers do. Or are supposed to do.

My generation (I was born in 1980) is the last to know the survivors of the Holocaust, to know them as grandparents, as great-uncles, and -aunts. I know them as rigid, parsimonious. Frightened. They are old, but they seem to have always been old. They count the matches in matchboxes, save teabags for second and third steeps. They raised families, they continue to raise grandchildren and great-grandchildren, as if to replace the dead. Lind was not like them. He could never settle down; he abandoned women, divorced wives. He scraped by, drank, smoked cigarettes, marijuana. Psychological treatment intended to exorcise wartime memory included LSD experiments intravenously perpetrated by a certain Dr. Ling; this was in an era when no English-language magazine or newspaper could refer to London without calling it "Swinging London," the latter 1960s. Macho, mustachioed Lind was garrulous, and, once published, famous. He summered in Mallorca, negotiated unsuccessfully with Hollywood. When in New York he stayed at the Chelsea Hotel. How many survivors were also hippies? How do you say "hippie" in German? *Hippie*. (Though "flowerchildren" sounds more menacing, archaic: *Blumenkinder.*)

Not all translations are so perfect, however. Lind writing in English, which he did from 1969, was yet another "Lind"—displaced from German, distant from its slangs, forced to the cooler imagination of what was his fourth fluent language (German, Dutch, Hebrew, English). If the enduring *Soul of Wood* was the beginning, *Ergo* marked the end of his fictional promise, and only memoir could follow, written in a knowing, polished version of what London's German-speaking "expatriates" called "Emigranto"—what Lind once referred to as "DENGLISH oder ANGLO DEUTSCH." *Counting My Steps*, *Numbers*, and *Crossing* were those memoirs. The other, slighter, novels were *Travels to the Enu* and *The Inventor*, which went almost unreviewed. In the 1990s Lind got sick; good friends and editors died by the year. Before Open Letter decided to bring them back into print, the only available English-language copies of Lind's novels were used: $1 each, over the Internet; two memoirs I purchased for that sum at Manhattan's Strand bookshop had even been autographed ("To Albert," "To Alfred").

A draft of this introduction was written as an essay for *The Forward*, intended to mark Lind's 80th birthday; it was published a week before his death. Three or four people (older, huskily-voiced women) phoned me after that, telling me how kind Lind was to them in New York, how funny he was, how they regretted they "never got around to reading his novels." But fiction followed by fact that must, in turn, be followed by silence, disappearance, neglect, and regret is a reduction we readers cannot accept, or allow—though that might have been the daily-felt fate of the writer. "Jakov Lind" doesn't just deserve to be read; he's necessary, both in the vicissitudes of his life and, too, in the work he created. His books are a late bloom of the European Jewish landscape, straining sunward through the concealing concrete.

Joshua Cohen
12/2008
Brooklyn, NY

LANDSCAPE IN CONCRETE

I

There is a plague called man.

WHEN YOU LOSE YOUR WAY in the Ardennes, you're lost. What use are plans and prayers. A landscape without faces is like air nobody breathes. A landscape in itself is nothing. The country through which German Sergeant Gauthier Bachmann was making his way on the second Monday before Easter was green but lifeless. He rattled the stick in his left hand over the tree trunks, they stood as close together as fence posts. To the right of him unplowed fields stretched out to the horizon. A sultry wind blew from the south, driving larks and other small birds, drying the puddles in among the clods, and coming to rest in the branches. Bachmann was heavy and shapeless, like the blanket of clouds that covered the fields. His lips were as dry as the bark of the trees, his stomach as empty as the plains. He saw only what thrust itself into his field of vision: the pointed fingers of thin branches, the green hair that welled from the ground, brown pustules that seemed to be made of earth, entrails that looked like roots. Hunger made him as light as a feather. This was the beginning of his fifth week in the Ardennes. Something had to happen—and it would have to be soon. Where there are fields, there have to be people, and where there are people, army camps can't be far away. The thought of army camps full of brisk and sturdy soldiers twisted his mouth into a smile. He looked for a gap in the ranks and found one where he had least expected it. In the very first rank. Morning roll call. Count off. One, two, three, four. The voices were sharp. Heads snapped to one side. Twenty-one, he yelled. Twenty-one. Sergeant Gauthier Bachmann of the Eighth Hessian Infantry Regiment. Reporting for duty, yessir.

The wood to his left swallowed up the echo. Sir, sir, sir, he shouted with all his might, baring big yellow teeth on the final "r." The wind dispersed the sound. His boots scraped over the ground like a dull plow. The day showed every indication of being like the ones before it. He clenched his teeth and risked a jump. And then the unexpected happened. From a hole in the ground no bigger than a fox's burrow popped a creature with his finger pressed to his lips. Pst, pst, he went, and a man, small, dark, and skinny, crawled out of the hole, shook his fist in Bachmann's stomach and yelled: You're caving in my entrance, you damn fool.

Get away from me, you! Bachmann was scared stiff. He hauled off and poked his stick into the ghost's side. It writhed with pain and made faces. You've hurt my kidney, the critter whimpered. Good, said Bachmann and got ready to strike again. Then it dawned on him: the ghost spoke his mother tongue. You're not a mole?

Me a mole? Are you crazy? I'm a German.

A German? Bachmann wasn't going to be made a fool of. He was delirious with hunger. In such a state, he knew, all sorts of things can happen. The critter held his side and limped around him in a circle.

You're a liar! Whish! He tried to shoo him away, but the little fellow kept nimbly beyond his reach. Whish, Bachmann went, get away! He spun around, brandishing the stick. How can it be a German? Must be some cross between a man and a beast, like those mongrels that sometimes get born in out-of-the-way places.

But I am a German. We talk the same language, don't we? The argument had its effect. Standing by the entrance to the burrow, Bachmann lifted his right boot. Don't, the other cried out. Don't do it! That's my home! His home? ran through Bachmann's head, then he must be lying. That's no kind of home for a human being. He brought his right boot down with full force. The boot vanished in the ground. The construction was frail, further proof that the whole thing must be a trap. Something pulled him downward. The little fellow's head grew smaller and his hands shriveled. But his legs kept growing and growing. Bachmann disappeared below the surface of the earth as in a tomb. When the ground was up to his chin, he climbed out again and dusted off his clothes.

The little man was sitting under a tree, quaking with the cold, as if somebody had routed him out of a warm bed at night, and looking wide-eyed at this monster whose uniform was just as ragged as his own. Say, that was clever of you, that was pretty smart! He still couldn't take it in. He'd really unearthed a human being. The little fellow was squatting like an Indian. Pointed knees were growing out of his ears. The human sitting posture was conclusive proof. What's your name?

Xaver Schnotz, my company is over there. He pointed in the direction from which Bachmann had come. You know that? Bachmann was amazed. You know that and you stay here? I didn't see a thing. I haven't met a soul in a whole month. If it weren't for the planes, I'd have thought I was dead long ago. The Elysian fields.

Don't insult the fields, said Schnotz. Without these fields I'd have been dead long ago. Do you realize how warm it is down there?

No.

Plenty warm. You're a stinker. You've wrecked my house. But I won't go with you. If you keep on going, you'll be at the border by tonight. Without me. I'm staying here until it's over. Have to dig myself a new hole. It's too risky in the hut.

Hut?

Too risky, I tell you. It's up against the wall for the likes of us, or the noose.

Bachmann stood up: I'm beginning to catch on. You're a deserter.

Sure, what else.

And I thought you were lost. So you're a deserter. That's great.

Schnotz detected something wrong in the tone.

What do you mean: So you're a deserter? What are you, a Wehrmacht patrol?

Not at all. But I'm not a deserter either. Not by a long shot. The opposite. I'm looking for my regiment.

I don't get you.

Oh yes, you do. I'm looking for my regiment. And if I don't find my own, I'll join another. Been on sick leave long enough. High time I was doing something.

Schnotz was thunderstruck. He must be pretty far gone. Or he's an informer. Crazy idea. They wouldn't send out an informer like that.

Now I get it, said Schnotz. It takes all kinds. Something's wrong with you?

No, said Bachmann resolutely. I'm perfectly all right. But there's something wrong with those people on the medical board. They claim my nerves are shot. Tell me the truth, do I look it?

Schnotz looked the enormous Bachmann over from top to toe. He didn't see anything wrong and besides he didn't want to mess things up. He could smell the bread through newspaper and coat pockets. He guessed there'd be more edibles in the knapsack. No, he said, I've seen crazier people. You look perfectly normal and healthy to me. What are you going to do?

Let's go over to the hut, I'm all in. We can take turns standing guard, and there we'll at least have a roof over our heads.

There isn't any roof, only a few rotten planks, but I'd like to look and see if the peasants haven't buried some kohlrabi, they do that around here.

Schnotz ran ahead or in back like a dog, he kept pointing his ears and making faces. Bachmann had cut himself a new stick. With Schnotz cutting capers around him, he strode deeper and deeper into the woods like a Goethe on his Easter promenade. He felt almost human, at least he hadn't felt so stimulated in months. He kept having to interrupt his account of his plans with an "Over here, over here." Schnotz was as nimble and nervous as a weasel. He chewed on a blade of grass and squinted up at Bachmann from time to time. His hand to his left ear, his gigantic Adam's apple bobbing up and down. What Bachmann was telling him struck him as so implausible that he didn't trust his ears. Plan A, said Bachmann, is maybe the simplest. I creep into an army camp at night and hide in the cellar. I wait for a fresh batch of recruits to turn up, and as soon as I hear them marching through the gate, I pop out. I wait till they're in the shower room, naked everybody looks alike. Then to the quartermaster's, I draw a new uniform, and I'm in the clear. Sure, I lose my rank, but I get a second chance. That's worth the sacrifice. What I need is an old camp building with as many passages, rooms, and storerooms as possible. You don't think much of it, I can see that by your face. Plan B. Combat situation. It's hard to get there. There are sentries, patrols, and manned trenches all over. But once you've broken through, you're in the clear. After that you just have to show you've got what it takes. I'm no coward, friend, you can take my word for it. Mortars and such things don't scare me. The more noise there is the better I like it. You don't know me. The only part I don't go for is wet trenches and mud. Aside from that any kind of terrain suits me. Once the fighting is over, I lay my cards on the table. I tell them frankly who I am—but they reward me for bravery in battle. My discharge is canceled. It stands to reason; because I proved I'm a man, I showed them I've got what it takes. I'll even come in for a decoration. But that's not what I'm out for, don't get that idea.

Schnotz had climbed up on a branch, he'd thought he'd heard strange voices. But when he realized it was only the echo of Bachmann's voice, he jumped down and ran after him.

The hut's over there, Schnotz whispered, sticking his head into a clump of bushes. Bachmann gave a start but quickly pulled himself together. He wasn't going to let the sight of a peasant hut interrupt his train of thought. Plan C, Schnotz, may sound fantastic. But it has its points. Would you kindly cut out sniffing and running around? Listen to me, you can learn a thing or two. I'll need a military cemetery. I pick out a suitable spot between two graves and bury myself. Like you in your fox burrow. Only I can't afford to leave such a big hole. The air shaft mustn't be any bigger than a waterpipe with a diameter of two and a half inches. Otherwise people would notice it. So I lie in this grave and wait for a funeral. I'll need about a dozen people in civilian clothes. Uncles, aunts, parents, and such. As soon as the services start, in between the priest's blessing and the sermon—before the visitors and relatives have recovered from their emotion—I rise up out of the grave. Anyone who sees a soldier in uniform rising out of the grave is bound to stand up for him. People can't say no to a soldier with catalepsy, that's a safe bet, they're too sentimental. And what does the man want? Nothing, except to be marked fit for active duty. He wants to join his buddies at the front. It's sure to work, there's only one possible hitch.

The technical arrangements have to be made with precision. If something goes wrong with the air shaft, the consequences can of course be tragic. Because if you really die in the grave, you'll be dead and buried when the funeral starts up, and all your work will be for nothing.

That plan is terrific, said Schnotz, who happened to have been listening, you've got to try it. When you come out, the people will be so scared they'll make in their pants. So even if you don't succeed, you won't have to worry about anybody trying to kick you.

Schnotz had found a beech tree and was looking for beech-nuts. He crawled on all fours. For lack of teeth, he had to crack the shells with his fingernails. He looked like a squirrel.

Plan D, Bachmann announced. A column of soldiers is marching down the road. A thousand men, two thousand—row after row on their way to the front. I hide in a cranny in the wall near a curve in the road, and when the sergeant's view is cut off, I fall in. As if it were the most natural thing, I just march along. Hup hoop hip hore, keeping perfect step so's not to attract attention, only buttoning my pants as if I'd just been taking a leak. Not a bad idea if you ask me. Or I could jump on a moving train, why not, and just mix with the men.

That's a good one, said Schnotz chewing on a nut, very good in fact. Too bad you don't want to join the navy, I'd have a suggestion.

Really? asked Bachmann.

You swim after a battleship and crawl into one of the torpedo tubes. That way they won't see you. And when they start firing, you'll be the first to go. You'll be right in the thick of action. You'll get a medal.

Bachmann didn't like to have Schnotz making fun of him.

Schnotz was already sitting in front of the hut, he had actually found a hole with turnips and sugar beets in it, and was stuffing his pockets. I've got another idea. Why not report to Major von Göritz. He's stationed less than twenty miles from here. If you've got a pencil, I'll show you the way. Tell him you don't care about women, but tell him in a diplomatic kind of way, and he'll take you right in. Naturally you mustn't tell him you met me, or I'd be washed up. They shoot deserters. You know that. Bachmann found a pencil and let Schnotz sketch the road on the back of his book. It seemed like a long way, but in the last four months Bachmann had put longer distances behind him. Thanks, he said, that's not a bad idea. I'll keep at him, don't worry. I'd like to feel human again, that's what I'm really after, I'm sick of being an outcast, see what I mean? But I won't have anything to do with the other thing, it's against nature. It's perverted. What else could I do for the guy?

Von Göritz? He kept a Belgian for a while, but you can't offer to bring him back, except his dead body.

What happened to him? Bachmann wanted to find out as much as possible about this Göritz, the modest beginnings of a plan began to take root in his brain as firmly as spores in humus. Future mushrooms.

The Belgian was a cook, a civilian. Nineteen years old. Then somebody poisoned him out of jealousy.

Cooks don't get poisoned every day. Bachmann eyed the other distrustfully. Dusk was coming on, and Schnotz managed to hide in the gathering darkness. You couldn't get a good look at his face. Only his nose protruded like the beak of a bird of prey between deep-set burning eyes. This was a different Schnotz from the one he had seen earlier in the day, peering out from the hole in the ground. In his eyes there was no fear but a dangerous flickering fire. Those were the eyes of a fanatic. What had happened? Bachmann wanted the whole story and no double talk. Though he was twice as big as Schnotz and at least three times his weight, he rather feared him, as he would a vicious, venomous insect. Major von Göritz was a man of honor. You could bank on his word, a man of incredible ability. When he moved into the theological seminary with his guards battalion, the place was a mess and smelled like a stable. Before leaving, the priests had broken all the windows, scraped the surface off the walls and every single table and chair, smashed every tile and piece of glass, and shat into every corner of the building. You never saw so many piles. The whole place stank like a third-class toilet in a railroad station. When we moved in, I was there from the start, we had to take out the shit with shovels and wheelbarrows, even on the top floor. For three weeks there was nothing but shit. We worked in gas masks. We burned almost two hundred pounds of incense, we found a whole room in the cellar full of incense, the brothers must have been hoarding it. Do you think it helped? Not a bit. You couldn't get rid of that stink. So help me, friend, a Belgian seminary. But von Göritz was terrific. From the very first day he set his men an example, he dove into the shit just like everybody else, like a common private, you won't believe me, friend, but I saw it with my own eyes. It didn't get him down, in fact he was always bright and gay. He set an example all right, and how. The kind of German you and I admire. He didn't care a shit— in every sense of the word. Two months later the place began to look like a human habitation. The rooms were clean and newly furnished, we helped ourselves to a whole furniture factory, the windows had been repaired, and everything sparkled with cleanliness, the way you and I remember from home.

Did you get a new bathroom? Bachmann interrupted impatiently.

Just wait, I'm coming to that. Von Göritz wasn't satisfied with the freshly painted walls and the newly furnished rooms. He finagled skilled workers and the necessary supplies, the man has amazing organizational talents, used to be in the hotel business, and had a kitchen built, brand new, freshly tiled from floor to ceiling, the workmen had to admit they'd never seen anything like it.

What about toilets? Bachmann broke in.

The kitchen was completely automatic. Even in wartime it

was possible. But it takes a von Göritz. Nobody else could have done it. Well, first of all there were the potato peelers, presto change-o, press the button, turn on the water, and ten minutes later two hundred pounds of potatoes are all peeled. No dirty hands, no stiff arms. There were machines for cleaning carrots, for cutting up cabbage, and now you're going to think I'm pulling your leg: there was a machine for shelling peas, beans, and so on. Isn't that something? Yeah, that's something, Bachmann admitted.

And there was one more thing, he sent away to Paris for it: a soup mixer. A tremendous pot of course, made of shining new aluminum, naturally. You put in your meat, your parsley, your carrots, kohlrabi, chives, salt, and pepper. Dry, as is. Then you put on the lid. And you press a button. Only one button. The lid seals itself hermetically on a rubber washer, the water flows into the pot, just the right amount (he stressed these words), you sit down beside it and read a book. While you're reading, and that was the only chance we had to read, the water heats to the boiling point and in twelve to eighteen minutes, depending on the quantity, the heat shuts off. A bell rings. Man, the soup is done! (In his excitement he shouted the last words.)

In eighteen minutes you've got soup for four hundred men. And no dishwater, man, the finest meat soup. That's amazing, you'll have to admit. More, said Bachmann with glassy eyes, more about the kitchen. I won't tell you any more about the kitchen, that's enough for me. Bachmann heard the melancholy in the voice, you couldn't miss it. Schnotz rubbed his hand over his stubbly beard (which for some reason refused to grow properly) and tried to wipe away a tear unnoticed.

What's the matter?

Nothing, said Schnotz.

And you won't tell me any more about the kitchen, or about the new toilets and bathrooms. Well, if your description is on the level, I'll soon be able to see with my own eyes if you haven't been handing me a line. (In his heart, of course, Bachmann didn't doubt the story. How could he have doubted? He'd have had to dream up another kitchen and another army camp to take the place of Schnotz's lies. And he'd never have been capable of that.)

Schnotz didn't want to say any more. He was busy with a turnip and possessing only his two right canines and a third isolated tooth in his upper jaw, he had to scrape the turnip to make it digestible.

Bachmann tried to make him talk again, for under the very unusual circumstances silence struck him as dangerous.

So naturally, Schnotz, he made you chief cook and you worked the button of the soup pot, that couldn't have been so easy, naturally you must have had pretty good connections.

His voice became honey-sweet.

Let's not talk about it any more, Bachmann. Is that really your name?

Don't worry, I'm on the up and up. You can trust me, you were head cook, weren't you?

He locked me up, Schnotz sighed. Locked me up in a cage with iron bars and a feeding dish. He (he stressed the *he*) fastened me to a chain. He put manacles on my ankles, to keep me from running away. But he didn't put the chain on properly. In three days I was gone. Too bad.

Too bad? Several mushrooms were sprouting at once in Bachmann's brain. Too bad? That means he cleared out practically against his will, how much will would it take to bring him back? He made a special note of the "too bad."

What for, Schnotz? You don't get locked up for no reason. What did you do?

I, I poisoned the Belgian bastard. With piptol.

Piptol?

That's right. He didn't deserve any better. And piptol works, and how. Piptol is terrific. No cackling and howling like with arsenic. Have you ever seen the way arsenic affects people? Arsenic is all wrong. It sticks to your fingers, three weeks later you still have to keep washing your hands. Or cyanide. Cyanide is stupid. If you get a whiff of it, you conk out yourself. And it's much too quick. No, piptol's the stuff. Piptol is O.K. Your eyes crawl out of their sockets like snails and they can't get back in. (He tittered.) Your tongue gets stiff and hard as shoe leather, black leather, and your nostrils contract so tight you couldn't stick a needle in, they close up as if there'd never been any holes, your ears hang down like dry leaves, and your hands cramp up like this, they turn into claws (he demonstrated, tittering again), and then, very very slowly, you suffocate. That's piptol, friend.

And you did that, Bachmann asked in horror. He felt his nostrils contracting. Why did you do it?

Night lay over the two of them like a black blanket. Without answering Schnotz stood up, a thin beast of prey, and crept to the doorway (the door was missing). A man who uses piptol is capable of anything, you can't let him out of your sight. Bachmann followed him. The first impression is always the right one, this proves it. Bachmann stood in the doorway and saw only shadows, the darkness was almost complete. And as he dreamed drowsily into the darkness, he saw it all clearly. Plan E illumined the night inside and the darkness outside like the Northern Lights: Schnotz goes back to von Göritz. Out of gratitude von Göritz takes Bachmann in. What could be simpler? There's a plan without any hidden traps. He repeated: Bachmann brings Schnotz to von Göritz. He has a reward coming to him. What would I like in return?

He smiled. No need to answer such questions. A kitchen with white tiles from floor to ceiling. He smiled wearily. A lid that seals hermetically on a rubber washer. Just the right amount of water. Push only once, it says here in black and white. Once, not twice.

Read for eighteen minutes, maybe stretch it to twenty-five. With twenty-five minutes' reading I'll finish the last ten pages. He'd been saving up the last pages of his book *The Gold- and Silversmith* for three years, though that's the most important part, the summary. Twenty-five minutes. The bell rings. You can smell the meat soup from one end of the occupied territory to the other, it tickles the noses of the boys at the Atlantic Wall, who have to live on haddock. Congratulations, Bachmann. Thank you. He's secretly put in ten pounds of meat. For his buddies. Bachmann's done it again. Gauthier is O.K. May I sit next to you, Gauthier? Say, Bachmann, can I bunk with you? Congratulations, the soup is really first-class. Thanks, boys. I do my best. Before they have time to eat their soup, a call comes through the loudspeaker: Surprise attack! Go to it, men! Not without Gauthier, the men shout in chorus. We won't fight without Bachmann. O.K. Bachmann, you lead them! It's an emergency. He takes off his apron, exchanges his white hat for a helmet. They run like the Furies, mow down every single Russki, and recapture the position. They keep going, with Bachmann in the lead—then comes the mud and they all drown. Every one of them this time—but it's not his buddies in the swamp, it's meat and carrots. Back in the kitchen, where it's warm and cozy, a clean body, no fumes like in Voroshenko. A tiled womb—you know where you're at. Nobody needs to be ashamed of me. Everything's like in the old days at home, only better. When my father's soul runs into another soul in the cemetery at night, my father asks, have you read the *Duisburger Nachrichten?* It's on the front page. The giant who held the front at Voroshenko was my son. Died like a hero.

Something grunted at Bachmann's feet, he gave a start and

looked down at the little pile of human shit that called itself
Schnotz, touched it with his foot to convince himself that the
shell wasn't empty, and yawned. If it weren't so late, I'd have
taken the guy under my arm and marched right off to von Göritz.
Here, Herr Major, I'm bringing you an old friend. I wouldn't
refuse a little favor in return. I have technical skills. Pushing
buttons is my specialty.

But it was nighttime, and at night he was determined to be
careful. A little fellow like that can wriggle out from under your
arm and before you know it he's up a tree (he's done it once
before). Schnotz had drawn his bare feet up into his pant legs
and his hands into his sleeves. He'd buttoned his jacket or what
was left of it over his nose.

He gave him a little kick, Schnotz let out a grunt. Bachmann
was sleepy but afraid to stretch out beside the insect. He still has
this one tooth. The tooth is poisonous. While I'm sleeping, he
crawls around on me and bites me. Bites my hand. The left hand
leads straight to the heart. How can you apply a tourniquet in a
hurry when you're half asleep? Does he poison everybody? He
bites my hand or maybe he even punctures the artery in my
wrist. Just my luck, meeting people like that. Even if there are
two sides to every calamity. This time, for instance, you could
hardly call it a calamity. This little stinky Schnotz is good for a
reward. All the way from the filthy hut, overgrown with weeds,
he could smell the clean army camp. Schnotz went on snoring
peacefully as if he were home in bed. The stinker thinks he can
snore while I'm batting my brains out? Don't make me laugh.
He kicked him again, harder this time, the little man still didn't
stir. If force won't do it, try kindness. Schnotz went on snoring,
or maybe he was only pretending. Just wait! He took his last
piece of army bread, removed its newspaper wrapping, and held
it under the snorer's nose. The smell of the bread woke him up,

he propped himself up on the palms of his hands and (lacking the strength to wrench it out of Bachmann's hand) looked up at him imploringly. Good dog, you don't have to stand on your hind legs. I only want to know the reason why. Out with it. Why did you poison him?

He couldn't see the man's eyes, but he had a physical sensation of the gnawing in his bowels, the spittle overflowing from his mouth. First the answer, then you can take a bite.

Go on, why did you do it?

His hunger pangs made Schnotz sneeze.

So you won't talk. All right. Bachmann took a bite himself and purposely made loud, smacking sounds. When his mouth was empty, he repeated slowly: Want a bite? How about it? Insidious silence. So you won't talk. A pigheaded poisoner. O.K. He raised the bread to his mouth but to give Schnotz a last chance waited before biting into it.

Schnotz opened his mouth, a torrent of passionate words poured out:

Peter, Göritz I mean, promised me the job in the kitchen. It was the job everybody wanted most. Obviously. And why me? Because I'd earned it. I was his, you know what I mean, call it his friend. I did everything for him, really everything. I'd have gone through fire for him. That's not what he wanted. He made you attend him front and back. Oh well. Besides, I was one of the first in the battalion, I had certain rights of seniority. Nobody questioned that. Of course Schnotz would get the job. They were all willing, even Mürz. And Mürz is ambitious. He had his own candidates. Anyway, Mürz was agreed. Then like a flash of lightning the news breaks. The job goes to this jerk Leo, he doesn't know a darn thing about cooking, and anyway he's a civilian. I ask you! You think I've got no feelings? Schnotz isn't made of stone. Everybody sympathized with me, even Mürz. They were all flabbergasted, they all bitched, but you know how it is, nobody did anything. There was nothing they could do. So I had to do it. I had no choice, and when Leo kicked the bucket, nobody gave a shit. They all had an idea who had done it. Göritz chained me up, but he did such a rotten job I was able to get away. Nobody cared. But naturally they put the blame on me. Can I have a bite now?

Schnotz bit violently, but he couldn't get it down so fast. Satisfied with the story, Bachmann let him take two bites and gave him another little piece extra. He ate the rest himself. To leave no room for doubt he tore up the paper. The scraps fluttered through the room and settled on the floor like white spots. After the last crumb Schnotz took a breath: So now you know what's what—piptol, oh, it's good stuff. Tongue? Like leather. Nose? Buttoned up. Ears like an elephant's. Teeth loose, ready to spit out. Eyes out in front. Liver all mushy like a rotten watermelon. The blood that flows back into the heart is all poisoned. Flows up and down through all the arteries and veins, eating up the blood cells one by one. That's why it's so slow. It took twenty-four hours before he was dead, piptol—good stuff, Schnotz tittered, holding his hand coyly in front of his mouth. Especially in breakfast coffee. When you get up out of an officer's bed all warm as toast, you want hot coffee. Warm body and hot coffee go together.

The coffee is first-class again, he said, and licked the last drops from the corners of his mouth. And then his tongue went stiff.

Jealousy, jealousy . . . I'm not personally acquainted with it, but I've known such people. Now Bachmann was ready to lie down and sleep. He slowly seated himself, spread his coat on the floor and put his knapsack at the head end.

And another thing, said Schnotz, now carried away with enthusiasm. Piptol isn't so very expensive. I'll tell you a little secret. You can make it yourself out of crushed blackthorn leaves. You take . . .

O.K. That'll do. Now I want to sleep. Save your story for another time.

For a while he lay on his back staring through the rafters at the night sky. Plan E shone on his tired eyes, a rational, geometric constellation like the Great Bear.

Too bad, too bad, Bachmann dreamed, there's nothing I can do to help him. He talks himself onto the gallows, he even expects people to take pity on his stupidity.

He saw letters and mathematical signs on the rafters. The sky, the walls, the woods, the Ardennes, the whole world and the universe were full of signs. $G + S - S = G + B = B + R = RB$. A rational Bachmann. I gain my reason, and he loses his stupidity. The signs are symbolic. If they don't mean more than meets the eye, nothing has any meaning. He read them again: $G + S - S = G + B = B + R = RB$. Not a letter or sign too many or too few. The equation is perfect. His mind at rest, he fell asleep.

ALTHOUGH HE ENJOYED FALLING ASLEEP, he spent a miserable night. He scratched, he slapped his legs, forehead, and chest. Beetles and spiders and, in among them, little Schnotz (so he dreamed) were crawling all over him, biting, pinching him, and refusing to be caught. It didn't really surprise him that he couldn't catch Schnotz, because Schnotz had left a snoring dummy lying in his place, while he himself went hunting small animals in the woods. He could see him clearly: black, naked, and dirty (the dirt is camouflage) on a branch. Crawling after a squirrel, holding it by its bushy tail. And then he vanished. Then Bachmann saw himself rummaging through the autumn leaves. He found Schnotz lying on his back and hit him in the face with his stick. Then he was gone.

Tired with searching, Bachmann woke up. He stepped out of the doorway, stretched, and rubbed the sleep out of his eyes. The grass and the autumn leaves were covered with dew, birds were screeching, and it was cold. The bundle of rags behind him was snoring. If a Schnotz in the hole was a surprise, a goose in between the trees was a miracle. It stretched its neck, sniffed the air, and poked around for worms that weren't there. No mistake, it was really a goose.

Bachmann sweated with excitement. Schnotz, a goose! Schnotz, a goose!

The fifth week was starting out promisingly. Monday a man in a fox burrow, Tuesday a goose in the woods. What will tomorrow bring?

Schnotz cursed and rolled up tighter than ever. Suddenly he uncoiled from the window like a spring. A goose! A goose! Quiet, Schnotz, quiet. He whispered: a goose!

30

Schnotz was speechless with excitement. He stroked his lips, he opened and closed his eyes with his fingers.

The goose about-faced. It hadn't figured on the two of them. Schnotz did a somersault for joy, hopped and leaped into the air, pretended he was going to let it escape, spread his arms and ran like a dive bomber, making engine sounds. Before Bachmann had budged, Schnotz had the bird by the throat. He squeezed with all his might, the goose screamed, unwilling to surrender to this eagle. It thrashed at Schnotz with its whole body, stemmed its feet against his chest, and hammered his nose with its beak. Hurry up, quick, give me your bayonet, Schnotz yelled. He hadn't expected the bird to fight back. Bachmann stood motionless while white and black wrestled on the ground. The knife, the knife, Schnotz shouted. Quick! Bachmann held the bayonet in his hand, he stood bewildered, he didn't want to give Schnotz the knife. The mere thought of warm, fresh blood turned his stomach. No, I can't do it. Let her go. Let her go? Are you crazy? I'll eat her alive. Give me that knife, you coward. Coward was too much. And he couldn't stand the cackling and screaming any more. Bachmann felt pity for the Lord's poor creatures. Their blubbering broke his heart. Poor dumb creature! (He felt no pity for Schnotz or for himself.) Here, said Bachmann, and handed the bayonet to Schnotz, who was fighting on his back. Here, do what you like. He turned around so as not to see the blood and he held both ears so as not to hear the last cry. He heard a high loud croaking like a human voice, and then a buzzing. A high, long-drawn-out organ whine that took a long time to die away.

Hell's bells, said Schnotz to his prey, you pretty near got me. You fought bravely, you were all right (he gave him an appreciative tap on the beak), but it didn't help you. You can't do a thing against a knife. Steel is always stronger than flesh. One is cold, the other warm—cold always wins. Bachmann leaned his shoulder against the hut and heard strangely familiar music in his ears: Oh pain, oh smart, thou'rt breaking now my stricken heart. Thou'rt gone and fled, my sweet Body, my God, now Thou art dead. Oh Lord, forgive me. I have sinned. He crossed himself. Forgive me, my sweet Jesus, I didn't mean it. It's the war. Forgive me. War makes swine of us. Pater Noster. But no one's responsible. Our Father which art. He crossed himself again.

Schnotz dragged the dead bird behind him, saw Bachmann crossing himself, and without looking at him threw the bloody knife at his feet. Then he went inside.

Bachmann stood there a while, dazed at the sacrilege, then he picked up the knife, wiped it in the grass, and followed Schnotz. Dead things didn't bother him. Dead things were like stone or glass, they didn't remind him of anything living. If you could only get through the couple of minutes between life and death. Only a few seconds, that's all. But how?

Maybe I'm a coward, but cowardice is inevitable in critical situations, and death is a critical situation. Then you've got to stop your eyes and ears, or you're cooked. He put the knife down on the table, took off his cap, and started plucking. Schnotz meanwhile was trying to make a fire. O.K., said Bachmann (the plucking was done), now we get to work. He picked up the knife, but dropped it right away. It's so sharp, he cried aloud. The nail they drove through His feet must have been that sharp, if not sharper.

The fire blazed up in the fireplace. Make it snappy, you churchmouse, you pious stinker, Schnotz shouted, or my fire will go out. Bachmann wasn't listening. He saw the chunks of meat piled up on the table and more heretical ideas ran through his head.

They didn't cut the Saviour in pieces, but some of his martyrs they did. HE got off easy, but not the others. (Chop, chop went the bayonet.) HE hurried on ahead, bleeding and slightly punctured, but mostly in one piece. That's why they call him the Prince of Peace. Bachmann enjoyed these religious games. In religion he allowed himself to mix things up a little, an indulgence he denied himself in all other matters. He didn't dare to take any liberties with nature, he was afraid of nature.

Men can defend themselves, but what can animals do in this world without steel and dynamite? We can riddle any animal with holes and cut it up. With people it's different, I don't know why, but it's not the same. Men are men, they have reason and weapons.

And you're a donkey, said Schnotz, a yellow swine. If the goose had killed me, you'd have said your three Pater Nosters. You're a degenerate. Men are men, he aped Bachmann, but you're not one of them. You're going to come to a bad end. You'll be lucky if there's anything left of you, even shit.

Schnotz didn't look exactly human himself. Blood-spattered, feathers all over his cheeks. His scrawny neck scrawnier than ever, growing out of his collar like a withered vine. His neck had to carry a head that was too big and wobbled dangerously when he talked. His piercing black eyes, his protruding cheekbones in a face from which starvation had gnawed every ounce of flesh and fat, gave him, as it had the night before, the appearance of a fallen bird of prey. His nose was thin, flat and hooked—a vulture.

Me a creature? Me a donkey? Can a donkey suffer when a poor goose's throat is cut? A donkey has no pity. I'm not a donkey, but he's raving mad. And the consolation of not being a donkey reconciled him with Schnotz's nasty words. That consolation meant more to him than poking Schnotz in the jaw. While they were cooking the goose, the aroma appeased them, they concluded a kind of truce. Schnotz even grew talkative, he told stories about his life. He reeled off everything that came into his head and finally intimated with a titter that Göritz would give anything to lay hands on him, Schnotz. For a Schnotz at large, a Schnotz capable of telling a court-martial about Göritz's private life, would mean the end of the Major.

Plan E lay cleverly hidden behind Bachmann's white, bloated face. It lay beneath the roots of the blond fuzz on his all but bald skull and lurked insidiously in the nostrils of his stout Breughel nose. When the iron kettle with the steaming fragrant goose (cooked up in a broth with turnips and onions) stood between them, Schnotz suddenly had an idea: All right, Gauthier, out with it and don't lie to me: now that you know all about it, are you going to hand me over to Göritz? Bachmann hadn't expected that question. The truth, it occurred to him, is always more effective than a lie, and what interests me is the final outcome. The thought of that kitchen, that peaceful sanitarium atmosphere in the former theological seminary, drove him wild. Yes, said Bachmann, there's only one thing for me to do.

What?

I've got to take you with me. Why did you tell me all that? You twisted your own rope. I've got to be a soldier again or I'll go to the dogs. Didn't you know that?

Schnotz was silent for a moment. Then the words came slowly: No, that's something I couldn't have dreamed.

But that's how it is, friend. As soon as we're through eating, I'm taking you away. Schnotz laughed: Anyway you've got a sense of humor. I've got to hand you that.

First, let's eat. Who gets the liver?

I get the liver, said Schnotz drily.

No, Schnotz, the liver is mine.

Would you like my leg instead, take the leg.

No, I'm not interested in the leg.

The breast.

No, not the breast.

How about the neck?

Certainly not the neck.

What would you like then?

The liver.

The liver? Oh no, that's settled. I get the liver.

They glared in silence, they were ravenous.

What would you say to my wing?

Keep your wing.

Hell, wing is good.

I don't want a wing.

Skin?

No.

Heart?

Never.

Leg? Schnotz asked slowly.

I've already told you. And not your neck or breast or wing, either, but . . .

I know, Schnotz leaned forward and gave Bachmann a piercing look, I know: the liver. But that's mine. Is it my goose or isn't it?

It's not your goose, Schnotz.

I don't think I've got you straight.

I repeat. It's not your goose, Schnotz.

Then whose is it?

It's our goose. Yours and mine. Or actually the other way around. I saw it first.

Saw it, yes. But I made it into something edible. If it weren't for me, it'd still be cackling and you'd still be saying your prayers.

Prove it.

Schnotz stood up. He had taken courage, the courage of despair. See here, Bachmann, somebody's got to tell you. You're contemptible, repulsive, and cowardly. You're a coward. I've told you before, and I say it again. A coward. If it hadn't been for me, you wouldn't even have picked up your bayonet, you only carry it around for decoration, and you'd never have cut the goose's throat. Don't argue. If I hadn't killed the goose, you wouldn't even have had a wing, because living geese are no good to eat. Besides, they flap their wings. See what I mean, they're inedible.

Bachmann stood up too, and to give his words greater emphasis he went around the table.

I found the goose, Schnotz, I repeat, I and not you. You were still snoring, maybe you were even dreaming about this goose. But you can't eat the liver of a dream goose, Schnotz. You can die of hunger in your sleep, it's been known to happen.

Impressed by his own speech, Bachmann sat down and relished his enemy's confusion. Why does he go on arguing, he wondered, in twenty-four hours Plan E will be carried out, and he'll be sitting in a cage. Schnotz, who had suffered humiliation all his life because of his feeble puny body and no less because of his name, wasn't concerned with the liver, but with the principle. He had fought that goose to the death—to deny him his reward was an insult, a slap in the face. Bachmann, on the other hand, wasn't the least bit concerned with the principle, but only with the liver, for one good reason: he was especially fond of goose liver. Another consideration may have been that he wasn't going to take orders from a deserter and pervert. In a calm, deep, and almost weary voice he said: Don't you touch that liver.

The liver, Bachmann—Schnotz tried on his meanest smile and gave himself an air of having dreamed up a really sly stratagem—will be mine to eat and no one else's.

Maybe, said Bachmann, casting a forceful look across the table out of his small lusterless eyes, maybe some other time. But not today.

He reached into the iron kettle, past the liver, took his wing and started smacking his lips. To rile Bachmann, Schnotz reached in too, touched the liver provokingly for about two seconds with the little finger of his right hand. Then he took his wing . . .

They ate in silence, occasionally wiping the juice off their mouths with their sleeves, and looked at each other.

Schnotz contemptuous and challenging, Bachmann serene and self-assured. Bachmann had the larger teeth (by comparison Schnotz's toothless mouth ground very slowly) and was through with his wing in a few minutes. He played with the little bones in his right hand and waited. He glanced into the pot and even let one eye come to rest on the liver. He smelled the broth, registered the daggers in his adversary's eyes, and still didn't reach in. But when he raised his head, Schnotz, quick as a salamander, reached past Bachmann's nose, grabbed something brown, and looked up smiling. Bachmann's anger did him good. But it wasn't the liver he was chewing on, it was the heart, and he kept spitting out bitter pieces. Bachmann broke the breast into two halves and took his share. The breast kept him busy. He removed the thick layer of meat and bit into it like a sandwich. Schnotz took his leg and the other half of the breast, made as if he were going to say something, but said nothing, because silence struck him as slier than speaking, and only belched. Then he gave a broad grin.

To Bachmann bad manners were the true sign of low origins.

You and I are cut from different wood, said Bachmann. At home in East Prussia I bet you people shat at the table.

That's right, said Schnotz. We're only plain peasants, it's perfectly normal. But we kept Rhinelanders, they had to get down on all fours, we used them for benches.

Watch your step, said Bachmann, I'm of Flemish descent myself, but a Rhinelander wouldn't take kindly to such remarks.

But that's the way it was back home. We used Flemings, male and female, for farm horses.

You've got a pretty loose tongue on you for a man with only twenty-four hours ahead of him. Do you realize how painful it is when the rope is too thin? That can be very unpleasant. Besides, the jiggling gives you heartburn.

He reached into the pot, took his leg and in two bites had devoured everything but the bone before Schnotz had finished his half breast.

Nothing was left of the goose but two piles of bones, they spooned up the broth, sometimes with onions, sometimes with turnips. Lonely as a foundling, the liver lay brown and fragrant in the pot, as forsaken and innocent as a dead soul. Schnotz and Bachmann held their hands on the table edge; sprinters before the starting gun, motionless, hypnotized by invisible eyes. A cuckoo called in the wood.

Bachmann swept away something invisible with his hand, Schnotz misunderstood the gesture and instantly his hand was in the pot. Like a long hairy pair of tweezers his thumb and forefinger dipped in—but he had underestimated Bachmann's strength and presence of mind. Grabbing Schnotz by the wrist so hard that he screamed, Bachmann raised his left hand, reached into the pot, seized the liver and popped it into his mouth with the speed of lightning. It happened so fast that Schnotz saw nothing but distended cheeks and tight-pressed lips. It being a good-sized liver, Bachmann couldn't move either his tongue or his jaws at first. His hand still gripped his enemy's wrist. Schnotz tried to tear himself loose, but escaped only by bringing down Bachmann's elbow on the table edge with all his might. He held his aching wrist. Bastard, he hissed, bastard.

Bachmann was unable to answer, the liver stopped his mouth, he held the back of the chair with his left hand and felt armed. He chewed slowly, but watched the other closely. His almost lifeless eyes observed the other's slightest movement. You'll pay for this, if it costs me my neck. You're going to be court-martialed. Bachmann had just swallowed the last morsel, he licked the corners of his mouth and said in a very loud voice:

Not me, Schnotz. You're the one that's going to be court-martialed. He opened his belt buckle. Wise up, Schnotz, wise up before it's too late. Admit you're a fool, a half-wit, you've put yourself in my hands. I can do what I like with you now. And because I can do what I like, I'm going to be generous. I won't hand you over. Schnotz said nothing. His silence floated between the two of them like icebergs off the coast of Greenland. You could feel it hammering against his temples, you could feel the lust for vengeance nestling in the hollows of his eyes under his low forehead, tugging from within at the corners of his mouth and pulling them down. His legs wobbled.

You look like an old Hun, Bachmann chortled. The East Prussians are really Poles if not Mongols. You look like Satan in person. You're a riot.

Schnotz was silent. Bloodlust lurked like a vulture in his innards. If I bite through the bastard's stomach, he thought, I'll get my liver, even if it makes me sick. Injustice must be paid for. Your days are numbered too, said Schnotz, clutching the inside of both sleeves with his fingers and rubbing his nose with both sleeves at once. I'll tame you yet, you'll dance like a circus horse when you feel my spurs.

Bachmann felt the spurs in his hips and the iron of the bit cut into the corners of his mouth. His chest heaved, the down on his scalp blew in the breeze. He turned horse completely, and now he was a horse he could trample anybody underfoot. Certainly this Schnotz. A kick in the stomach, a kick in the head, a leap over the fence, and off and away into the open fields.

Let's make peace again, Schnotz, he held out his right hand, but for good this time. The liver is in here, he pointed to his stomach, and to give his words emphasis, he overturned the empty pot. He kept his hand outstretched.

Schnotz pushed the hand aside. You won't have any peace with me, not now or as long as you live. You were stronger and quicker, and that's why you've got to pay. Brute force has got to knuckle under. Every horse has to belong to a man.

Don't you talk about men, you no good bum. Your hash will be settled quick, I'm not letting you out of my sight. I've thought it over, I'll let mercy prevail over justice, I won't take you with me. For my money you can stay here and starve. As soon as I get to von Göritz everything will be all right with me. So thank your stars. Plan E can wait. Tomorrow morning I'm shoving off—without you. Meanwhile let's saw some wood, so we don't freeze tonight. He pushed Schnotz out the door with one hand. The saw sang with the shrill voice of a bird, the logs fell to the ground with a dull thud. They plied the saw with might and main and looked past each other. Schnotz, who with every tug of the saw cut off a chunk of Bachmann, saw blood dripping to the ground, Bachmann heard angel voices in the choir of the church of St. Nicholas at the Berner Arch. He was pleased with himself. He had won and forgiven the vanquished. He had sacrificed his own plan and practiced charity like a good Christian. Life was good again, it was a remote childhood in a sailor suit, it was a flower bedecked team of horses on the way to First Communion, a seat between father and mother, a white scarf and a candle decorated with ribbons, it rang like church bells and smelled of incense. The taste of the wafer on his palate, candy-sweet and yet a trifle bitter, like a liver, a strange taste, nothing tasted as good as the bittersweet body of our Lord Jesus Christ. With tears of compassion the Madonna holds the Holy Child (my mother never held me that well, even as a baby I was too heavy)—mercy and kingdom come, amen and hallelujah for all eternity.

The louder grew the jubilation within him, the heavier he felt, his intoxication was too overpowering to last, it ebbed, it

drained off like bath water, and in the end his joy turned to a
bestial melancholy from which there was no escape. He'd have
liked to run away, the impending afternoon held sinister prospects
in store for him. It wasn't Schnotz's fury and vengeance he
feared, but his easy victory over his enemy, his own strength
and dexterity. The sadder he grew, the more sluggish became his
movements, and finally he stopped altogether. He left the saw
wedged in the wood and sat down. He propped his head in his
hands and sat there, hearing and seeing nothing of what was going on around him. The noonday was sultry. Regular snoring
issued from the hut. He stood up and crept in for his knapsack.
Though he had been expecting just this, Schnotz didn't wake up
right away. It was only after going some two hundred yards that
Bachmann heard a scampering, a rustling and coughing behind
him.

THE FORMER THEOLOGICAL SEMINARY, now occupied by a guards battalion under von Göritz, was situated in a large well-kept park, at the end of a broad avenue. The peace and seclusion of the place suggested a sanitarium rather than a military installation. When Bachmann and Schnotz presented themselves at the gate, the sentry rang Master Sergeant Mürz asking him to come out and arrest Schnotz officially—at his own request. My goodness, if it isn't Xaver! Won't the chief be pleased! You won't believe me, Schnotzi, but we'd given you up for missing, we thought you'd starved to death. Yesterday we saw your smoke. I said to the chief, Herr Major, there's smoke going up in the woods. Should we take a look? Forget it, he says, don't bother me with that cripple. What do I need a poisoner for? (Schnotz went deathly pale.) He'll kick in all by himself. And now, Schnotzi, you nitwit, we'll have to shoot you. Well, it can't be helped. And now get moving. Back to your cage!

Schnotz was led away under triple guard. Bachmann and Mürz sauntered along behind him over the raked gravel path, past flowering magnolia bushes. When they came to the building, Bachmann couldn't help himself, he followed the kitchen smell. The kitchen was in the cellar. The windows were open. Not only was the aroma overpowering—roast pork—but the tiled walls, the immaculately clean tunics and hats of the kitchen staff, and most of all the freshly polished aluminum pots all but took his breath away. The stone flags of the floor, so clean that they mirrored the pots, made him weak with joy. The sight of this model kitchen gave him a glorious sense of security. So he wasn't lying, said Bachmann, it's even more beautiful than I imagined. Lord, how beautiful it is. Here I'd like to stay. Come along, said Mürz, the chief doesn't live in the kitchen. If you want to see him, you got to make it fast, or he'll close up shop. It's almost closing time. Did you find Schnotz, or did you just happen to run into him? He's got something coming to him. Turn Schnotz in and stay with the regiment, said Bachmann, that was Plan E. You could say that it developed all by itself.

Mürz looked at the giant suspiciously: Go on, he said, you were smart. Have you got the same tendencies as Schnotzi? No, not I, sergeant, I have no tendencies at all. My regiment's disappeared and I'm looking for another. So far I haven't had any luck.

Sure, sure, you giant, you've got a good build on you. So you need a regiment. We'll fix you up. Would our guards battalion suit you? It's nice and quiet here. Bachmann looked at Mürz, his voice trembled, and he clutched his hand: If you could do something for me, Mürz, I'd be eternally thankful.

You bet, said Mürz, disengaging himself from the handclasp. Then he delivered Bachmann to the chief.

HERR VON GÖRITZ LOOKED SO WELL-GROOMED that he might have been taken (in civilian clothes) for a hotel manager. He was a man in his middle thirties with a short, well-cut face. His blond hair, wavy at the sides, smelled discreetly of violets. He gave the impression of a pleasant, cultivated man. With shrewd, nervous eyes he surveyed Bachmann who sat before him with cap in hand like a petitioner. There was no sign of homosexuality in von Göritz, his well-groomed exterior was not effeminate. His voice and gestures were quite masculine and normal. The pleasure he took in dealings with young men was the result not of any physical disposition but of intellectual arrogance. He couldn't bear women because of their stupidity, they bored him. There was nothing complicated about his relations with men, he changed them like shirts. He had been married for twelve years, a happy childless marriage of convenience (his wife was a doctor and like himself had inherited a private fortune). In civilian life von Göritz was a real estate administrator (he held a degree in engineering). The news that Schnotz had been brought in had irritated rather than angered him. Living or dead, the fellow was a matter of utter indifference to him, like the regiment, his wife, and the war. Of all things in life this war was the most repugnant to him. Its motives were idealistic, that is, irrational, unrelated to victory or defeat. He saw war as full employment with disastrous consequences. A kind of schoolboy roughhouse, culminating in nothing but bloody noses and torn clothing. He favored no ideology or philosophy and was opposed to all religions and mass movements. Stupidity offended his esthetic sensibilities. He looked on the whole world around him with the same ironic smile as he now wore in examining Bachmann's

44

papers. He handed them back and said: Oh well, you're due to be discharged. There's just one thing I don't understand: what are you still chasing around here for? Why don't you go home?

My regiment, Herr Major, it vanished off the face of the earth in Voroshenko, it drowned in the mud as if it had never been there. It was simply gone. When I woke up in the hospital in Oppeln, it was gone. I'd have let well enough alone if I'd known it was *final*, that it would never rise up again. But then the day they took the bandage off my head, somebody in the next bed said: Bachmann, that's rubbish. A whole regiment can't disappear. It's only been decimated, but they must have patched it up afterward. So it still exists. That you're still alive proves nothing.

And that's the truth. That I'm alive proves nothing. God has given me a second chance. I've got to do my duty. God, if you'll forgive me for saying so, has singled me out. I have chosen you, my dear Gauthier, to prove yourself a second time. Your comrades are dead, so this time you must try and see if you can't succeed in dying. That's why I don't want to be discharged, that would be insane.

Von Göritz understood at once that he was dealing either with a clever dissimulator or with an unfortunate victim of the battlefield. Pleased with his exordium, Bachmann leaned back in his chair. We all have our Voroshenkos, von Göritz said, I mean our lost battles we escape from by the skin of our teeth. We have no business tempting fate a second time. Be sensible, try to forget the whole business. Forget? That was the lowest, most brutal suggestion of all. Forget Voroshenko? He could feel Voroshenko in every fiber. Each one of his organs was a hill or a valley, each one of his blood corpuscles was a dead comrade. Forget Voroshenko? Never as long as he lived. Yes, if you could tear open the earth and call all the fallen back to life, if you could turn that parcel of Russian soil inside out like the lining of a coat—then gladly. Then I'll forget Voroshenko.

We can't stand the world on its head for you, Herr Bachmann. And just imagine what confusion there'd be if we raised all the dead, don't you think there are enough people as it is?

I can't judge that, Herr Major, said Bachmann with a voice from the tomb, I have no firsthand knowledge of that. But in any case, there's a war going on right now, isn't there? And in wartime I want to serve like everybody else. I could go back to my trade, I have a good trade: gold- and silversmith—we're descended from an old family of gold- and silversmiths. But would that be right? Originally we were Flemings. From Ghent. My first name is French, and I'm a German. That makes me a real European. Germanic and Aryan to the core. Not a drop of the wrong kind of blood. Besides we're Christians. Devout Christians.

You couldn't do any better, said von Göritz and suddenly had an idea. This fellow might come in handy. What have you got in your knapsack?

Bachmann removed the contents of the worn-out knapsack slowly and carefully. Von Göritz leafed through the book, *The Gold- and Silversmith,* published by Anton Graussbart in Göttingen in 1907. A textbook for students at the Dresden School of Applied Art.

An excellent book, Herr M

Isn't it a little out of date?

Not in the least. These things don't date. Recently, it's true, they've obtained excellent results in Munich with nickel steel electrodes, but the Heppler alloy is, and remains, the soundest method. Heppler can't be praised too highly. It's true that a certain admixture of F_2B and basalt dust is inevitable, but that doesn't impair the gold content or the sheen in any way. Malleable fine gold, we might as well face it, is still very much in demand, and it offers two advantages that shouldn't be underestimated: a high degree of brilliance and minimal waste. What more can you ask? Point two percent isn't much, is it?

I haven't the faintest idea, Herr Bachmann. No, point two percent can't be very much, that much seems certain. And von Göritz had arrived at another certainty: This giant is a conceited fool who wants everybody to like him.

Can you shoot?

I've got the gold sharpshooter's badge, Herr Major. That ought to be good enough. He displayed the badge.

The badge is genuine, said von Göritz drily, you've convinced me. I'll make you a proposition, Sergeant Bachmann, though I can't promise you anything, give us a sample of your marksmanship tomorrow morning, and if everything goes well, maybe I'll let you stay here a little longer. If you're really any good, there might be a spot for you in our battalion. I can't make any promises and you are under no obligation either.

The beginning is always hard, Bachmann thought, but at least it's a beginning. If he can use me for hunting, he'll end up keeping me here for good. That kind of thing can always be arranged, if it's done from above.

Rabbits or partridges? Bachmann asked. Just say the word.

Neither. Von Göritz stood up. First he looked out the window at Sergeant Mürz, who lay smoking in the grass, faithful to his master and waiting to be called. Then he turned to Bachmann.

Neither rabbits nor partridges. We'll start tomorrow with a Belgian who will be executed for sabotage and high treason. Then the day after tomorrow we have a German soldier, a deserter. I can never find more than five volunteers, and Mürz is too expensive. I need six. Are you with us?

It's a beginning, Bachmann said to himself, and one good turn deserves another.

With pleasure, Herr Major. Traitors and deserters suit me fine.

Frankly, hunting rabbits and partridges doesn't appeal to me. The poor things.

Then I can count on you?

Yes, sir. I've been getting out of practice. For the last six months, I've just been traveling around.

And what did you do in the woods?

Ate goose with Schnotz. Xaver Schnotz. I think he knows you. But I got the liver.

You're all right, sergeant. And not as incurable as some people think. Anyway tomorrow morning. And then we'll see. Von Göritz tapped on the windowpane. Mürz threw away his cigarette and double timed around the corner.

Sergeant Mürz, give this man a bed and take him to the kitchen. See that he gets a good meal. I'm afraid we haven't any special beds for people your size, Bachmann, but I hope you'll sleep all right regardless.

Bachmann packed up his things in his knapsack, saluted, and about-faced. Saluting in itself gave him a sense of well-being. The elbow is bent at a 45 degree angle, the outstretched hand is raised to the hairline above—but never touching—the right eye. The soldierly, pleasant, and so typically masculine sensation induced by this posture did him good.

Just one thing more, Sergeant Bachmann, at ten you'll find me here over a glass of beer. It's a muggy evening. I invite you to join me.

MUGGY, HELL, SAID MÜRZ on the way to the kitchen. Faggy is more like it. You've started up pretty good with the major. (You're not as dumb as you look.) He wants something out of you, like to bet.

Really? Bachmann asked.

Yes, really. And I'll tell you something else: Tomorrow morning you're going to knock a man off. Am I right? Horning in on my business. Never mind. But it's not very nice of you.

Why, what do you mean?

Don't be so innocent. Have you any idea what a headache I have rounding up five volunteers every time? It costs him five hundred marks a throw.

Bachmann was extremely pained at having antagonized Mürz so unexpectedly. He tried to make up.

But see here, Sergeant, I'm only obeying orders.

Bachmann, it was easy to see, had no experience with offended Austrians. An offended Austrian must never, never on any account, show a conciliatory attitude toward the offender, even though he usually forgets in three seconds who has offended him and why. Accordingly Bachmann failed to see why Mürz should be growing steadily more malignant.

You can't pull the wool over my eyes, you think I don't know your kind? You think Schnotz didn't tell me all about you? The act you put on to get away from the front, and how smart you were, always managing to tuck yourself away in some mental hospital.

But then they got your number, they were going to send you back, so you showed your true colors. You sneaked into a shower room and attacked a couple of minors, so they'd put you down

49

for a pervert. But it didn't get you anywhere. Then you pinned on some phony medals and played Napoleon. Then you raped an officer in the train and claimed he owed your father something. And when all that didn't help, you hid in a soldier's grave until they dug you up and gave you a kick in the ass. I have to hand it to you, you got plenty of ideas.

Bachmann was indignant: it's not true, that's a lot of slander. The major asked me, I couldn't turn him down.

You want to shove off tonight? You crazy? Nothing doing, you'll leave here when we want you to. You've taken on this job, now you'll have to go through with it.

We've got good healthy air around here, said Mürz as he was turning to leave, almost like Semmering. Only it doesn't agree with everybody. Enjoy your dinner.

THERE HAVE BEEN SOME CHANGES since this afternoon, Bachmann. I've petitioned the supreme commander of the Western front to pardon the German soldier. In other words, there may be no more work for you the day after tomorrow. Bachmann was sitting on a little iron chair beside von Göritz. That's a bad beginning, he mused. The beer didn't taste right, and he couldn't see much sign of the wholesome air Mürz had mentioned. Everything smelled of violets and cigars. It was a bright spring night. On the chestnut trees white blossoms lay like snow. A stray plane buzzed in the sky.

My petition for the Belgian has been turned down, and my men aren't very experienced. Von Göritz paused briefly. I'd like the man to die from one shot, in the middle of his heart.

Just like this. He stuck a match through an empty box, it made a slight crackle. Just like this, Bachmann, at the first shot.

I've got the gold badge, Herr Major.

The distance is fifty paces, Sergeant.

That's no distance.

I don't want him to suffer, is that clear?

A traitor and saboteur?

But a friend. What I'm telling you now I'll deny later: He set off an explosion that cost 235 German soldiers their lives . . .

Horrible, Bachmann interrupted.

Not in the least. Plain justice. 235 rats the less. It's the Belgians' country. We're intruders.

Permit me to interrupt you, Herr Major. 235 soldiers are 235 human beings. A murderer is a murderer, even if his motive is political. The 235 left 235 relatives. Hundreds of orphans

51

who weren't to blame for the war, any more than the men themselves. I can't understand your sentimentality.

It's perfectly possible that you don't understand, Bachmann. But we have no feeling about hundreds, especially if their cause doesn't mean anything to us. With an individual it's different.

Because he's your friend.

Because he's my friend. Exactly. You're free to choose. Do you wish to take part tomorrow or not? I can't save him.

Why, certainly. The man deserves to die.

You'll hit him straight in the heart . . .

You have my word.

I'll show my gratitude. And now good night, Sergeant Bachmann. Von Göritz stood up. Bachmann also stood up. They shook hands. Von Göritz went in. Bachmann sat down again. He mulled things over: They make him a major. Homosexual, effeminate, sentimental, and people like me get sent home. No wonder the whole front is cracking up. The decline of the West has already begun. Anyway, I've got to get up at five.

CHRIST ALMIGHTY, WHERE ARE MY SHOES? I shouldn't have taken them off. The jeep was outside the window and all the men, including Mürz, had climbed in. But Bachmann couldn't find his shoes. They were supposed to be in the quarry by five-thirty. Hey, Bachmann, Mürz shouted, shake a leg.

Bachmann leaned out the window. My shoes are gone.

The men in the car had to hold fast to their rifles, they were doubled up with laughter.

It's no joke, Bachmann yelled, my shoes! Somebody's swiped them. The laughter grew louder.

He crawled under all the beds, rummaged through the lockers, looked in the trash baskets. No sign of any shoes.

Mürz stormed into the room and shouted: It's five-thirty, what did you do with your shoes?

Put them under the bed.

And somebody stole them. Is that what you're trying to say? See here, soldier, I don't like your attitude. You've only been here one day and already you're making trouble. There's no thieves in this outfit, Mürz roared. Here, try these. He produced a pair of shoes from behind his back. Maybe they'll fit you.

Well, thank the Lord, Bachmann sighed. That's them. They're mine.

Oh no, brother, they're not yours. Somebody left them standing here. But you can have them for ten marks. I'll put it in the Christmas savings box.

Ten marks? For my own shoes? He sniffed at them. They're mine. I swear they are.

Shut up. They're not yours. Ten marks. Make up your mind. You can't report in bare feet.

53

He put the second shoe down in front of Bachmann.

They look so familiar.

Shoes always look familiar. It's twenty minutes to six.

But I haven't got ten marks.

Doesn't matter, put them on quick. You'll owe me.

Bachmann put the shoes on. I don't like to run up debts.

Everybody has debts. You can't serve on a firing squad with bare feet. It's not allowed. You owe me ten marks and you'd better pay up soon.

The car sped downhill over a narrow logging road, then jolted over several miles of open fields. A hill came in sight, surmounted by chimneys and iron frames, and off to the right of it lay the stone quarry, white and steep like the cliffs of Dover. Next to Bachmann sat fat little Kaiser, coughing incessantly. No reason, he coughed, why your whole day should be ruined for ten marks, after breakfast we're off duty. Don't take it so hard.

I still don't get it. Last night I put my shoes under the bed, and this morning I have to buy a pair. I'm not crazy. I'm not going to pay for my own shoes.

No one answered. Only Kaiser, who felt the need of distraction, said: You weren't wearing any shoes. I noticed that yesterday as soon as you came in.

I wasn't wearing any shoes? You're getting me mixed up with Schnotz. He was barefoot.

How could anybody get you mixed up with Schnotz?

The men grinned. Mürz turned around and said: Instead of being glad that I find you a pair of shoes, all you do is cry on our shoulders. You'd think ten marks were a fortune.

It's the principle, sergeant, the principle.

You with your principle. Here we are at the quarry. First let's get to work, we can talk later.

A LITTLE MAN WHO LOOKED strikingly like Schnotz, though half his face was hidden by a blindfold, leaned trembling against the white wall as Mürz read the sentence. When he turned around, the figure looked familiar to Bachmann. The sentence (high treason, sabotage) didn't apply. They raised their rifles. The figure by the wall slumped, he was almost kneeling. Bachmann broke out in a sweat. I promised to put a bullet through his heart, he suddenly froze with terror, I promised more than I can deliver. He aimed below the left shoulder blade. I can't do more than that. If he doesn't die at the first shot, it's the end of my career. Mürz is bound to report it. Fire! somebody cried. Bachmann pressed the trigger. He lowered his rifle and went pale with fear: The others hadn't even raised theirs. The six of them were staring at him without a word.

You said fire, Bachmann stammered.

I? Mürz asked. I said fire? I was only telling the boy here he looked tired. Now look what you've done. His feet carried him to the wall. The six pressed behind him. When they came to the fallen man, Bachmann's eyes looked for a way out, but all he saw was low-hanging branches and above them a gray sky. His escape route was cut off. Mürz had turned the body over with his foot, he knelt down and took off the dead man's blindfold. It was Schnotz and he wasn't dead, but dying.

Kamerad Schnotz. Bachmann knelt beside the dying man and closed his eyes. Kamerad Schnotz, they've taken us both in. He crossed himself, folded his hands and began to pray. Not quite dead, Schnotz moved his lips, Bachmann clasped his hands and bent down close to the lips, his nose touching Schnotz's left ear. Then he stood up and moved on, praying.

What did he say? Mürz yelled behind Bachmann, what did he say? Bachmann didn't answer. He went on praying.

While three of the men carried the dead Schnotz to the jeep, Mürz, hands on hips, stood behind Bachmann and roared at him. I'm in charge of executions around here, see? Ask my men. You think I'm going to let a newcomer take over? You don't know me. Murderer! What did Schnotz say? he added more calmly.

That's my secret. Our Father which art.

I read the order wrong, Herr Major, we shot Schnotz instead of the Belgian.

Schnotz? Who's that? Calm down, Sergeant Mürz. Oh yes, Schnotz. The deserter and poisoner. We may have a very nasty business on our hands, Sergeant, I'm expecting a telegram any minute.

Bachmann couldn't contain himself another minute: in the first place he wasn't tied, in the second place the others didn't fire, in the third place they'd turned his face to the wall, how could I be expected to hit the heart?

What heart? asked Mürz. Nobody said anything about hitting his heart.

Let the man speak, Mürz.

In the fourth place, Bachmann cast a grateful glance at von Göritz, I was a little nervous on account of the business with the shoes this morning. Let me explain: My shoes were stolen last night and I had to buy another pair that look very much like mine. Von Göritz joined his hands at the fingertips: Bachmann, I think you'd better leave us. . . . At this moment there was a knock at the door and a soldier stepped in with a piece of paper. He handed it to von Göritz, who read it and set it aside. Just as I expected, Mürz, Schnotz has been pardoned. Yes, I think you'd better try your luck somewhere else. The men here are a very close knit group, they don't take kindly to newcomers. Sergeant Mürz, would you please look up the trains to Cologne?

Mürz left the room.

I'm giving you a second travel order, it will take you to Narvik. Lieutenant Hupfenkar is a good friend of mine. You'll find him at the Army Information Bureau, in the station. He can find a place for you in a special duty battalion. Give him my regards. The telephone rang. 12:10? Good. Cologne-Honnef at 8:32 A.M. He hung up.

You hear that, Bachmann, your train leaves in one hour. A man will drive you to the station if you like. He took two blanks from his desk drawer, filled them out, signed and stamped them, and handed them to Bachmann across the desk.

Von Göritz stood up: Well then, Bachmann, it's been a pleasure knowing you. He held out his hand. Pleasant journey and much success. I have a feeling you'll go farther somewhere else. It's rather dull around here for a man like you.

You don't need to help me, Herr Major. And I haven't decided yet whether I'll leave today.

Well, well, you haven't decided. In any case, I have work to do. Good-by.

It won't do to take everything lying down. He scowled—his face looked idiotic in the convex mirror of the glistening aluminum kettle. It was three times wider. I look insane. I can't let anybody see me this way.

On leaving Göritz he had crept—better keep out of sight—behind the gigantic soup mixer from Paris. He sat there for a time with his back to the wall and his legs outstretched. Let them try to throw me out of here. They'll have to smoke out the kitchen if they want to get rid of me. "In the kitchen I'm safe," he repeated twenty times. And the longer the quiet lasted (the three men of the kitchen crew were playing cards and had ignored him when he had climbed down to them with a "Beg your pardon"), the safer he felt. Von Göritz won't let him throw me out. He won't allow it. The way he cut Mürz short. That proves he doesn't set much store by him. Don't give up hope, that's the main thing, don't lose faith in the good in man. Or where will you be?

Bachmann! That was Mürz. He was very near, his shout seemed to cut straight through the soup. Bachmann! Are you nuts? For ten minutes I've been standing here looking at your pants. Come on out from behind that kettle. At the sound of Mürz's voice Bachmann suddenly lost all hope in the good in man. There's no point, he said to himself, it can only end in a brawl. That's what I've got to avoid. I'm so strong, I'll have a murder on my conscience if I let myself go. I wouldn't want that. That's what he wants, the dog. I'm not going to soil my hands for the likes of him, no, not for him.

He had some difficulty pulling his legs out from under the soup kettle. Mürz leaned against the wall with folded arms, beside him stood the three kitchen helpers (after the death of Leo the Belgian, Mürz had seen to it that not one cook, but a team of three, always appointed by himself, should officiate in the kitchen), held their cards in their hands and grinned.

Get out of here, said Mürz calmly but menacingly, and on the double! He motioned toward the exit with his head. Bachmann had to pass in front of him. Like a whipped dog he went toward the door, looking neither to right nor left. He covered the sixty-odd feet with calm, measured tread (to give himself dignity), his eyes downcast, he could see himself in the flags. As he grasped the door handle, a voice boomed out behind him: We're not running a sanitarium!

He turned around only once, when he was already outside,

and cast a last mournful glance back at his lost paradise, at the far end of which stood a monster that was doubled up with laughter and slapping its thighs.

It was a warm summer day, the park was fragrant with flowers. Every bush and every flowerbed had a little sign with the Latin name of the species. There are many different kinds of plants and flowers, each one has to have its name if they are not to be confused. The names aren't picked at random, they are part of an old tradition. Like the tradition of the Bachmanns. Even if they fade and die in the fall, they keep their names and dignity. Just like us. We're an old family too, but this phlox is still older. They've outlived Rome and the Romans and yet they've died each year. The eternal return, you can call it. The sentry was asleep. The gate stood wide open. Once outside, he began to run, he ran faster and faster and suddenly stopped to sniff at the air or listen to silent voices—as Schnotz had done. As if the dead man's soul had gone into him and taken its place with everything that had already died inside him.

The aroma of roast potatoes and fried sausages was wafted over the countryside, bringing the water to his mouth. But no Schnotz stuck his nose out of the earth. Nothing crossed his path. Along the highway, columns of vehicles and artillery were heading for the front. He watched them and the tears came to his eyes.

II

KEEP THE WHEELS TURNING FOR VICTORY. Victory in Europe. Germany is victorious on all fronts. Bolshevism is a threat to you and yours. Norwegian worker—defend yourself. Fight on to victory, shoulder to shoulder with your German comrades. For Europe—against Communism. Narvik, Main Station, Track 1. The only signs Bachmann couldn't find were the most important: The Army Information Bureau and the men's toilet. He was in urgent need of both. The platforms dead, the tracks deserted. There weren't even any scraps of paper lying around. Through the open rotunda he looked out into the street. A horse-drawn sleigh, out of which piled three air force men and a girl auxiliary. Muffled figures coming out of a store. The sign: Hotel-Restaurant KONGEN OLAF, and above it in the grayness a flock of gulls circling over the roofs, then suddenly, one after another, swooping down on the street. The snow seemed to stifle every sound. And then the stillness of a cushioned room, the bare colorless walls of a monk's cell, the silence of paradise. Every word spoken in the city resounded as from a loudspeaker. A foreboding of ice fields and eternal snow and a smell of seaweed, fish, and oil. Invisible but palpable. So this is Narvik. Bachmann was tired, sweaty and unshaved. For four days he had slept in stations, at tables and on benches, sitting and even standing.

He couldn't understand how he had got here and what for. Like a sleepwalker he stared into space, took a few steps and stopped still. The little knapsack on the giant's back seemed no bigger than a package of sandwiches. He had pulled down his cap over his frozen ears. With woolen gloves, from which all his fingertips protruded, he buckled his pistol belt. This was his

63

destination. That battalion must be somewhere in the vicinity. This was his homecoming, he was all atingle with anticipation and wanted to sleep.

Sudden cries of command cut through the silence. Then music, the stamping of boots, a marching song. Bachmann's heart jumped with joy. The music and the song sounded familiar, so did the tread of marching men. He went slowly to the grating which separated the platform from the street.

The column of soldiers was a disappointment. They were wearing black uniforms and caps that were much too high and had tassels on them. The insignia on the flags also looked strange. He didn't care for the tassels and the marching song wasn't German. What a fuckup, almost the same but not quite. They look like the Duisburg band. A bunch of workmen blowing horns on their Sunday off in the hope of waking the town up! Hell, that's no good.

A civilian in a gray coat, gray muffler, gray hat (who had been following him since he got out of the train) turned to him: That's our Free Corps. Good men. We can be proud of them.

You don't say, said Bachmann. The man looked up at him smiling. Red nose, Bachmann said to himself, pointed face. Mouse or rat.

Good men, the stranger repeated. This is the tenth of April. We're celebrating the day of our liberation.

Liberation?

That's right. That's when the first German troops landed in Norway. The day of reckoning. The end of Jewish domination.

You don't say.

Until then our country was ruled by Jews and Communists. Thanks to your Führer and our Premier Quisling we . . . His words were lost in a blare of trumpets. The Free Corps had lined up outside the station, they were blowing and drumming one song after another like the Salvation Army.

What's that? Bachmann shouted. The stranger didn't answer. Someone made a speech. At the end people shouted Heil! The stranger held up the flat of his hand and called Heil! Bachmann saluted.

After some more shouted commands the column moved off, the handful of onlookers disappeared, and the gulls swooped down out of the grayness. The music died away and the silence was deeper than ever. The civilian was still standing beside Bachmann as if they had been friends for years, making no move to go away.

Can I be of any assistance?

I'm looking for the toilet and Army Information. I'm all sweaty, haven't taken my clothes off in four days. Seems like four weeks. My back and knees itch. You can't scratch all over at the same time.

You tried though. I've been watching you.

It didn't work. You've got to undress or you can't get at them. And an unshaven face feels lousy. But the worst is the itching. Amazing all the dirt and soot that get under your uniform on a long trip! You wouldn't believe it. Sweat dissolves material on account of the high acid content. Have you ever had wool in your bellybutton?

The stranger shook his head.

It looks like absorbent cotton. But it isn't cotton, it's from my undershirt. Wool in the bellybutton isn't good for you, because, something most people don't know, we take in oxygen through the bellybutton. Sometimes we feel cramped and depressed, and we think it's the weather. No, sir, it's not the weather, it's the wool in our bellybuttons. My bellybutton is clogged. I've got to get it out right away. Your Narvik doesn't appeal to me very much. Doesn't seem to be much going on. Where's the information bureau and the men's toilet?

The stranger held on to his red nose for a moment. He rubbed it with his thick woolen glove, looked up at Bachmann with gray suspicious eyes, as though trying to figure him out. I'll go ahead, he said slowly. Come with me. They passed by the rotunda. The information bureau's in there, said the stranger, the toilet is further down by the tracks. I'll take you. First time in Narvik? Yes, the first time.

From here to the North Pole isn't far to go. That was a local joke.

Yes, that's a fact. But which North Pole do you mean? There are two, Bachmann laughed, geographic and magnetic. By dog sled it's a day's journey between them.

Haven't the faintest idea, the stranger shrugged his shoulders, never thought about it. Here's the men's toilet. Idle talk has caused a lot of trouble, Bachmann informed him, people shoot off their mouths. But if you ask them what they mean, they don't know. Army only, it says here, or I'd have asked you in, we'd have had a chance to talk it over. I'd tell you how I came to that conclusion. Speech isn't silver and silence gold as the stupid proverb claims, which reminds me, I happen to be a gold- and silversmith and I've had a good deal of experience with those precious metals. Speech is perfectly permissible, even praiseworthy and often important. But not aimless talk, only rational speech. Speech is an expression of reason and reason is the critical faculty that separates the important from the unimportant, the chaff from the wheat. You've got to think things out carefully and not open your mouth until you've drawn correct inferences.

Do you have to go, asked the stranger pointing at the door, or don't you?

Yes, I do, and Bachmann disappeared into the men's toilet.

The toilet was walled with white tiles. The floor was tile mosaic and so dirty that Bachmann didn't know where to put down his knapsack. Then he found a niche over the washbasin. The water came out cold. Ice cold. Same with the faucet with H engraved on it. But Bachmann, who believed in hygiene and reason as well as destiny, undressed completely and hung up all his clothes on the hooks in all three toilets. Except for his army shoes, he stood naked in the washroom. He inspected his yellowish teeth at length and decided to give them a thorough brushing. Then he began to shave. He had to run the razor over his face several times, because the soap wouldn't lather in the ice-cold water. Next began a long and elaborate washing and scratching and, of course, the removal of wool from his navel. Unable to reach the soapsuds in the middle of his back, he decided to take a little shower. There was no pitcher. He took off his left shoe and sock, put the sock in the niche, filled the shoe with water and poured it over his head. But since it wouldn't do to run around with one wet foot, he removed his right shoe and filled it with water as well. Turning round and round, he emptied them alternately on his head, singing loudly: Ring around a rosy, a pocket full of posies. The water ran under the door and out on the station platform. The stranger stuck his head in and saw the naked giant emptying his shoes over his head and singing "ring around a rosy." He was too flabbergasted to speak.

Shut the door, Bachmann yelled. The stranger quickly shut the door. You civilian you, Bachmann shouted, the toilet is for soldiers.

You're turning the platform into a skating rink, the other protested behind the door. None of your business, Bachmann shouted back. Ring around a rosy, a pocket and so on. If I feel like it I'll flood your whole Narvik till the water runs into your ears. Narvik is a German military zone. He sang at the top of his lungs:

> Green are the forests,
> white is the sand
> blond is my sweetheart
> from Heligoland.

The song did him good. It warmed him up. He was about to launch into a new one that begins with: The banner blows, the banner sings, my sweetheart waves, when the door was thrust open and there stood three men in uniform. Behind the three a small crowd. The stranger, the station manager, a few post-office clerks and ticket sellers.

Close the door, Bachmann yelled. You're causing a draft. Then he recognized the insignia of a lieutenant, snapped to attention and saluted: Sergeant Bachmann. Second Hessian Infantry Regiment, Eighth Battalion. Just arrived in Narvik. Ready for action.

Are you crazy? the lieutenant roared. What are you doing here?

Arrived from the Ardennes in a state of perspiration. Had to wash, beginning to itch. Danger of vermin, now eliminated.

The three men in uniform closed the door behind them. You're hardly a credit to the German army, Sergeant Bachmann. Such things make a bad impression on the population of the occupied territories.

I'm sorry, Herr Leutnant. I request disciplinary proceedings and appropriate punishment. He poured the water out of both shoes and began to dress.

Are you Lieutenant Hupfenkar?

That's right.

In that case I have a letter for you from Major von Göritz.

The name seemed to make no impression.

Bachmann repeated: I said Major von Göritz.

Get dressed and report immediately to the information bureau. Yes, sir. In the rotunda. Last door to the right or first
on the left. I know how to get there.

He leaned back with folded arms and looked by turns at
Hupfenkar and at his wet boots standing in front of the red-
hot stove. He was glowing and sweating and feeling very uncomfortable. This Lieutenant Hupfenkar was being much too
gentle. Instead of threatening punishment, he was treating him
like a patient, instead of chewing him out he had offered him
a chair. He's still young, Bachmann consoled himself. Those red
beardless cheeks weren't much to his liking, the parted hair was
too well combed. A well-meaning schoolboy, but not a soldier.
He's never smelled gunpowder. He swiped that Iron Cross
somewhere.

Hupfenkar read the note from all angles, turned it in his
hand, looked for something on the back, found nothing. Very
well, Bachmann. Tomorrow morning you will leave for Honnef.
There's a train at eight o'clock.

I beg your pardon.

I'd get you on a train tonight, but there isn't one. Smoke?
He held out an open box of cigarettes.

Smoke? No thank you. Disgusting habit, breathing in burning plants. He made a face, as though Hupfenkar had asked
him to eat horse droppings off the street.

Herr Leutnant, you are the same Leutnant Hupfenkar? I
mean, you've read the letter?

Yes, I've read it, you saw me, didn't you, and your papers
explain the rest. Care to read it? He isn't telling me any secrets.

He handed Bachmann the letter. He read: My dear Bernhard:
I wish to keep the bearer away from here for a few days until
certain things have been straightened out. When he arrives, you

can send him back again. He is stationed in Honnef pending discharge. Yours, Peter.

Oh, said Bachmann. Oh. And I came here to report for duty with your special duty battalion. After all the war's not over yet. Are you aware that I have the gold sharpshooter badge? Well, I have. What is there for my kind of man to do back home?

Wait till you get your discharge. I see by your papers that you're a gold- and silversmith. No one will prevent you from practicing your trade. A splendid trade.

Bachmann's voice trembled: Herr Leutnant. I speak to you as man to man. I'm a soldier. Six foot two. As healthy and strong as a horse. (He bared his teeth to prove it.) I'm twenty-five. The prime of life. Germany needs every man. It says so on every wall in big letters. We may as well be frank. Germany is fighting for her life. And you expect me to stand aside? Hupfenkar turned to Bachmann and looked straight through him.

Sergeant Bachmann, the sooner you get it through your head, the better it will be for you: You are irresponsible. Mentally ill. He'd heard those words before. It wasn't the first time.

That's a slander, a lie. Besides, it was only a preliminary finding. I've put in an appeal. My case is coming up on May 10. I am neither mentally deranged nor sick and I protest against such slander. To lend his words emphasis Bachmann would have liked to stand up, but he couldn't, without shoes he was naked.

Herr Leutnant. I did my duty before and am perfectly capable of doing it again. If it's God's will, I'm prepared to give my life. It's not my fault if I wasn't killed at Voroshenko. All my comrades were killed, I came off alive. A man can't be punished for being still alive, can he? No, I'm not sick any more than millions of my comrades who are fighting for their country right now. If I'm sick, so is all Germany, all Europe, the whole world. Today the whole civilized world is fighting Bolshevism (he began to shout in his agitation), and I, I'm ready to die, to die, yes, to make the supreme sacrifice! IS THAT MADNESS? Admitted I may have my idiosyncrasies. Admitted I'm inclined to melancholy and perhaps to thoroughness. But who isn't? Is that abnormal? Is that being sick? What's sick about me? Every German is like me, they all do what they can. Willingly or not. Duty is duty. Please send me to the special duty battalion Major von Göritz mentioned. Do I have to beg you on my knees?

Bachmann was out of breath, again he'd have liked to stand up and again he was paralyzed.

Your indignation may be justified, Sergeant Bachmann. But what you're asking of me is impossible. I'm sorry, I feel for you. (Bachmann had impressed him by his agitation and the earnestness of his words.) But? There is no but. A war can only be fought with sound men. The highest demands are made on every individual, it takes nerves of steel. We have to do things that may not be to our liking. Yes, sometimes we have to do violence to our own nature. Most of the duties a war imposes on us, Sergeant Bachmann, are revolting, let's face it, insane, and yet the soldier who performs them has to be fully responsible. That's the way it is, it can't be helped. There you have it. I personally regret that I can't do anything for you. The board of appeal is your last chance. Anything can happen in these few weeks. But why all this talk? I can't make you out. Go back to Honnef, find yourself a nice girl, get married—and live in peace. You probably know one already, said Hupfenkar with a wink.

I know one all right. A beauty. May I show you her picture? He rummaged around in his knapsack, found a picture of his girl friend Helga, and passed it across the desk. Well, what do you say?

Beautiful, terrific. You'll be a fine-looking couple.

She's a wonderful girl all right. Unfortunately she has a canine missing.

That can be fixed. I envy you, Bachmann, I envy you.

You envy me? Bachmann looked at Hupfenkar with suspicion. What do you envy me for? Helga or my so-called madness, or are you just saying that? Mind you, I say "so-called madness," because until the board of appeal makes its decision nobody has a right to speak of madness. Bachmann's little blue eyes glittered feverishly.

Why I envy you I don't exactly know myself, I'll have to think it over some time. You mustn't look at everything from the tragic side, they let you put in an appeal, didn't they? I'm giving you a travel order back to Honnef and rations. At eight tomorrow morning you clear out of here, that much is definite. Hupfenkar stood up. As far as he was concerned, the incident was closed. Not for Bachmann. He was completely befuddled. So the same old lies about me have found their way to the North Pole. So I was right, von Göritz is at the bottom of this conspiracy, and no one else. First he sent Schnotz into the woods to set a trap for me, then when he saw that I saw through his slimy game, he sacrificed Schnotz to silence a witness. Then he sends me to his little friend in Narvik to get me out of the way for a while. But now I see the lay of the land. Germany is governed by perverts. The idea is to get rid of normal men like me. First humiliate us, then push us aside, and in the end wipe us out altogether. A diabolical plan. Those doctors on the commission—Christ, the looks of them, one had a diamond ring on his right index finger. Another had a cigarette holder and a piping voice—the truth is dawning on me. I look too virile, too healthy for them—so they put me down as incurable. That's it.

They mark me sick because they're afraid of my health, they
want to replace men like me with weaklings. It's a sinister plot
to undermine German manpower, and conclude a secret pact with
Germany's enemies. I'm interfering with their plans. That's a
good one. They say I'm sick. What a disgusting word.

Thanks to the cold bath and the warm stove he felt better
than ever before in his life. Sick? Sounds like dead, only worse.
And what did this snotnose mean by nerves of steel? And violence to nature? What in God's name does he take me for?
Does this young whippersnapper with the Iron Cross think I'm
that kind? Against nature? Nature is the land. I know what
that swine wanted of me. Nature means mud, nature means
Voroshenko. Wanted me to lie down in the mud of Voroshenko
with my fly open. Mightn't have been so bad, the opportunity
was there. But man, was I weak, I was practically impotent. It
went down right away. How does this character know? Sure, he
knows everything.

Suppose I was weak in Voroshenko, that doesn't mean I belong to his club.

Nature, landscape. It makes me sad. Sick. Sure, sick. No, that
youngster isn't as stupid as he makes out. I've no heroic deeds
to my credit, that's the trouble. Haven't proved my manhood.
That's it. I've just done my bit, never anything outstanding, and
special achievement is what counts. With me it was just the
opposite, after Voroshenko I went further and further west, I
crawled home—and, when the unit was patched up again, I was
left behind. I've been left behind.

Something was dawning on Bachmann. Fear cut into him like
a dagger pressed against his chest.

Got to admit it. Being left behind is a kind of madness. It's
backwardness, idiocy, I'm an idiot. There's something dirty about
it, something that can't be washed away. It can't be, it can't
be. I'm just as rotten as those bastards who are trying to sink

me—an effeminate weakling—A COWARD, a slacker, whether they know it or not, *but not an idiot*. I haven't done anything outstanding. That's the trouble. No personal achievement. So they treat me like dirt, like an animal, like a sheep among millions of sheep. I'm a coward, I Gauthier Bachmann, who for three years did nothing but the daily work of soldiering. Nothing outstanding. Burned a few villages, knifed a few Russians in close combat, but that was all routine, nothing unusual. If that's all you've got to your credit, you don't dare to show your face. Kirov, ah, Kirov! That was something. Hupfenkar was cleaning his nails with a small screwdriver.

Herr Leutnant, I've just remembered. Kirov. One Sunday morning in Kirov we mowed down two thousand Russian prisoners, I repeat, two thousand, with machine guns. But I've got to admit it was more boring than horrible. There were six of us, we began at seven A.M., it was four in the afternoon before we were through. It took them all morning to dig their graves. You can't imagine the way they dawdle. Pamalo, pamalenko. Just like Russians. They sang the whole time. And how those boys could sing. Every last one of them a tenor or a bass. I've got a feeling for music. It was magnificent, the way they sang, the whole valley came to life, the trees vibrated as if a wind had blown through them. They sang like the gods. One song after another. At four o'clock the last one was down. We were supposed to make sure they were dead, we mostly didn't bother. Let the poor devil get away, we said, anyway we were dog-tired. Just the same there were two thousand, except for a few. Bachmann looked across at Hupfenkar, who glanced back without raising his head (now he was filing his nails). Up until then he had only told the story about Kirov to the medical commission. It hadn't made much of an impression, and this time again it seemed to have fallen flat.

What do you say to that, Herr Leutnant? He had to repeat

the question. Lieutenant Hupfenkar picked up his cigarette, took a deep drag and put it down. He blew the smoke in Bachmann's face.

I'm billeting you at the Kongen Olaf, the hotel right across the street. But no more shenanigans, or you'll hear from me. He stood up and tucked away his nail scissors and file in a little leather case. Dismissed. You lucky bastard. He held out his hand.

When he finally had his shoes back on—they were still damp—he stood up. I guess those two thousand haven't done me any more good than last time. These young whippersnappers, no matter what you tell them, they always know something bigger and better. Arrogant swine. What do you think of that business in Kirov, Herr Leutnant? He had to know, of course it wasn't an act of heroism, but all the same shooting all those men wasn't exactly an everyday occurrence. If you hadn't, those two thousand men would have to share your rations. You weren't any too well supplied, were you?

Hell, no. We were starving.

Well, there you have it.

Lord, is he pigheaded, how can you get anywhere with a guy like that? But I know what'll impress him: I'll put on a battle of my own. How and where remains to be seen. But I won't let the grass grow. Fishwives talk, men act. Courage is like life, you've got to put it to the test every day. What you've inherited from your fathers, struggle to make it your own. The greatest of German poets said that, and it's true. A man has to show what he's worth, he has to look for danger and get the best of it. I fear neither death nor the devil. Who said that? I'm going to make my own battle, period. And when those medics meet on the tenth, I'll tell them all about it. Then *they*'ll understand that I belong, *they*'ll wise up. *I* belong, that's settled, a Bachmann belongs.

So once again, lots of luck, said Hupfenkar. Bachmann was far away. He looked out into space, through his eyes thirty generations of Bachmanns, of gold- and silversmiths, saw the snow and the dark grayness, as steep as bare high walls, which cloaked the Kongen Olaf, all Narvik, the whole world. In this world Bachmann was all alone. Hupfenkar saw only a gigantic figure and small blue eyes that reminded him of the glass marbles of his childhood. He only gained an inkling of Bachmann's private war and the heroic deeds he was going to perform when suddenly Bachmann shouted: I'll find my regiment notwithstanding. And notwithstanding we will conquer. To arms, torero, proud heart, victory is yours.

He slammed the door behind him with a loud crash and crossed the street with head high. He was nearly run over by a truck loaded with sailors. The driver stuck his head out the window and shouted: Where do you think you're going, you ass?!

Hupfenkar shook his head and smiled. He didn't envy the giant so much for his ticket to Honnef, he knew Honnef for a stinking hole, as for his lunacy. For him the war is over, he thought, little suspecting that Bachmann's war was just beginning.

To fight battles one needs two things: friends and enemies, and even in this respect Bachmann was in luck. His war had a chance to begin right across the street from the Main Station, in the Kongen Olaf. His friend was already waiting over a glass of beer. He'd followed him all day. This seemingly screwy German giant fell in with his plans, he wouldn't let him get away.

As soon as Bachmann's gigantic frame filled the doorway, the stranger who had so kindly escorted him to the men's toilet jumped up and came toward him.

It's really a pleasure, said the stranger.

You look familiar to me too, said Bachmann, didn't we have lunch together one time in the Cologne Ratskeller? That was, wait a second, exactly four years ago. You were the man whose wife ran away, and you've got two daughters, one of them's cross-eyed, but she has glasses now, and the other's in high school. Your father has lung cancer and wants to commit suicide. How is your father, is he dead?

My name is Hjalmar Halftan, said the stranger. I showed you the way to the toilet and I had to defend you against my own compatriots. They insulted you, it's as if they'd insulted the Führer and all Germany. I've taken all the names. They're going to wish they hadn't. Scum! A man's ashamed to be a Norwegian.

Why, of course, said Bachmann, incidentally my name is Sergeant Gauthier Bachmann. Second Hessian Infantry Regiment. Eighth Battalion. Gauthier is French. The name Hjalmar sounds familiar. Say, what are you doing here? Have you had that toilet cleaned? The floor is filthy. Disgusting.

Take a seat, said Halftan. Waiter, a beer, and make it quick. You're my guest. You're getting everything mixed up.

Bachmann sat down.

I have the same name as the President of the Reichsbank.

That's right, said Bachmann. Perfectly right. You remind me of somebody, but I don't remember who. He has eyes like a dog, and a wart. You haven't either dog eyes or a wart. The man I mean is in the police, charming fellow.

Thank you, said Halftan, but I'm not in the police, though maybe it looks that way because I seem to have time on my hands. No. I have more in common with my respected homonym than the name. I too am a genius in a certain sense. He looked up at Bachmann to observe the effect of his words.

Bachmann didn't stir a muscle. He looked down at Halftan, waiting for more.

Doesn't it strike you as odd that a man should call himself a genius?

Not at all, Herr Halftan. Excuse me.

He bent down over his beer and sucked up the foam. Halftan watched this operation with amazement.

The foam has to be taken off, Bachmann raised his head, and the truth is always admissible. If you're a genius, you're a genius. No need to be ashamed of your good qualities.

But who says I'm good? Maybe I'm evil, diabolically evil, an evil genius.

Halftan hid the lower half of his face behind his glass, the better to observe Bachmann.

That doesn't matter. Evil has its good sides too. And the wickedest of men is closer to the good than certain good ones.

Strange logic, Sergeant Bachmann, but not at all uncommon. I am an evil genius through and through and I have no trouble with my conscience. But I do have plans. Interesting plans. Perhaps you will let me regard you as my friend: As a friend, you can help me. I watched you all day in the train. I was sitting across the way from you. I like you. Would you like to be rich?

No. On the other hand I wouldn't want to be poor. We're an old family of craftsmen, the finest craft in the world. I'm a gold- and silversmith. We were originally from Flanders. My great-grandfather, Cornelius Beekman . . .

Come, come, Halftan interrupted, we haven't that much time. You're leaving tomorrow morning, I've found that out already, never mind how. So you don't want to be rich? You're right, there's no virtue in wealth. Only stupid people want to be rich. But you do want to keep your pride, isn't that so?

Pride, pride, Bachmann protested, took a handkerchief and trumpeted loudly, pride is nothing but a word. Nonsense. Simplicity. Simple is enough for me. Let me be a simple, normal, intelligent, human being. That's plenty.

So that's what you want to be. Halftan smiled craftily. He cleared his throat. You make a lot of sense. Only . . . simplicity isn't so simple. That takes explaining. Let's put it this way: If a man has too much sense, what could he do with his sense? Not much, my friend. He whispered mysteriously: Some crook will come around and steal his sense. There are plenty of crooks nowadays. It was different in the old days. No, take it from me. A sensible man stands a good chance of being deprived of his senses. Stupid people never get swindled, nobody bothers about them, it's the sensible ones who take risks. And they are always taken for a ride. Because there's always somebody who's still smarter. What you need, Sergeant, Halftan grew grave, isn't sense or sound mind, but . . . do you want me to tell you?

Right now I need my regiment and the decision of the board of appeal.

Right, cried Halftan eagerly and grasped Bachmann by the sleeve. You need self-esteem, self-respect. You have sense already. Your feeling tells you the right answers.

I need my regiment, Herr Halftan, my honor. He wearily wiped his forehead.

Right, and why? Because, said Halftan triumphantly, it will give you back the self-respect you've somehow lost. He was thrilled with himself, his nose glowed like a stove.

You see how it is, I'm a genius. He smiled. The regiment will come of itself, just be patient, but first you have to show your mettle.

How do you know that? Bachmann was excited. Who's been blabbering? How can you know that? Halftan laughed modestly: Nobody's been blabbering. I'm a genius. I can read people's minds.

You're right, Bachmann surrendered, I lost it, or it lost me. In any case we're not together any more. There's a war going on and they want to discharge me. I don't want to be discharged. It's insane. He looked around the room, as though expecting help from the walls or the lamps. The room was deserted, except for three German officers sitting by the window. Two elderly waiters were leaning against the wall. Their white jackets were dirty and frayed. They were looking, waiter-fashion, into the void. What am I doing here? This beer is no good. Bachmann stood up. But Halftan pulled at his sleeve. You're in Narvik, and you want to get back to your regiment. Is that right, Herr Bachmann?

Yes, I'm in Narvik. At the North Pole. It's full of snow around here, said Bachmann, staring at Halftan as if he had been a snow man, I wonder where it comes from?

From up above.

You're making fun of me.

Not at all. On the contrary, I take you very seriously. Waiter! Two cups of coffee, or would you care for a schnapps, we've got good aquavit here, buckwheat spirits . . .

No, thank you. No hard liquor. I never take anything

stronger than beer. Besides, beer is nourishing. Did you know that? A glass of beer is almost equal to half an egg.

Really? said Halftan. Half an egg. Anyway, you want to get back to your regiment?

Bachmann nudged Halftan and smiled slyly as though about to tell a dirty joke: And three glasses of beer are almost as good as two eggs.

Halftan, who was unfamiliar with German egg worship, looked blank. That's right, two glasses of beer. You know what I mean. They give you a shot in the short arm.

Beer or eggs?

Both, both. But never mind. Seven olives are an egg too, and a slice of roast with gravy is four eggs.

You don't say. Halftan knew nothing of such matters but attributed Bachmann's ability to talk about eggs as other men talk of sex to his eccentricity.

Beer can't help being bitter, but yours is sour. Phooey!

He stood up and reached for his coat which lay on a chair beside him.

Don't go! Once again Halftan clutched his sleeve and pulled him back down on his chair.

Sergeant Bachmann, you have stature and character. Before you go, allow me to drink to that. Human stature. You're a man. He held out his hand. Bachmann gave him five flabby fingers which the other squeezed with vigor and enthusiasm.

Yes, you are a man, skoal! He raised his glass, held it out toward Bachmann, tilted his head and drank.

A man. I'm a man. Man. How lovely that sounds. Every single letter smelled of jasmine. To be a man. He was stirred, intoxicated. It was as pretty as a Christmas Eve and sweet as glazed apples. It takes a perfect stranger, practically at the end of the world, at the North Pole, to tell me what I'd almost forgotten. I am a man.

Oh man, give heed, Bachmann recited so loudly that the waiters turned around, what does the deep midnight say? I slept, I slept, from a deep dream am I awakened. The world is deep, far deeper than the day had thought. Deep is its pain, deeper still than sorrow. Pain says: Pass away. But all pleasure demands eternity. Deep, deep eternity. Friedrich Nietzsche. Poems in the Appendix to *Thus Spake Zarathustra,* read them in the hospital at Oppeln during an air raid. Unforgettable. I am a man. A German man. He stood up and raised his coffee cup. When he sat down, there were tears in his eyes.

Beautiful, said Halftan and clapped. Like a true genius he had touched the right cord, the Bachmann countryside echoed trumpets and oboes.

What can I do for you? After this vote of confidence Bachmann was prepared for anything. I'll do anything you wish.

As often in northern latitudes, and the further north the more often, this Halftan was a kind of magician, he might almost have been an angekok. For this was exactly what he, the Nordic genius, expected of a Bachmann. Darkness, snow and cold and ice and the eternal fear of them are the right climate for magic and witchcraft. Hjalmar Halftan, who had grown up in this climate, struck while the iron was hot: The coffee can wait, he said coldly and stood up. I have a little car waiting two blocks from here. Come, it's late. He helped Bachmann into his coat. We'll take a little ride out in the country. There's somebody I have to drop in on, and you're coming with me.

He tossed some coins on the table and drew the bewildered Bachmann after him. They went out through a dark back door, climbed a few steps, crossed an empty billiard room, passed down a still darker corridor, and were suddenly out in the street. There's no need of our being seen, said Halftan. I'll explain the whole thing on the way. Maybe there'll be a bit of fireworks, maybe that can be avoided. And of course a slight risk is involved. But you'll have a chance to win back your self-respect. Determination, execution, success—that's what counts. He squeezed him into the car, which wasn't so easy. Six foot two and three hundred pounds make a pretty big portion of man.

They drove through deserted side streets. Halftan with his nose close to the windshield, Bachmann stiff and cramped beside him. His thoughts were far away. I'm a man, Bachmann repeated to himself for the hundredth time with a gloomy stare as if he had lost a dear one. To be a man, isn't that the best thing in life? His words were swallowed up by the roar of the engine. The car crawled up a mountain. Most of all, the country was white. The snow lay deep and everywhere. They drove along a narrow road high above the city. Behind roofs and chimneys, cranes, hangars, and warships, the sea glittered. Black and dangerous as an anesthetic. Ice and sea covered Bachmann's trees and thickets, concealed the chaos that lurked beneath. Flying over gray and white surfaces as the darkness deepened and the city receded, he began to feel good. In the snow from which nothing more protruded he thawed out.

He stretched his legs as best as he could, but his knees were still bent. His head touched the car top as though holding it up, he kept his hands deep in his coat pockets. This cradling, seesawing automobile ride with a stranger in the vicinity of the North Pole lulled him, but at the same time it made him fearful and strangely nervous, as though the cradling might suddenly stop. The car crept and panted up still steeper roads, his own weight seemed to press in the opposite direction. A few screws and wheels, strange iron and rubber shapes, are pulling me up a mountain. That's sorcery. He braced himself against the motion of the car, but the iron and screws were stronger. It must be the magnetism of the North Pole, Herr Halftan, I feel as if something were pulling me up.

We're headed south, said Halftan. He looked pale and tense

and was biting on his cigarette. It's the magnetic force of the North Pole, Bachmann was now thoroughly convinced, everything is being drawn upward, nearer and nearer and then . . . whish, it disappears into a hole. Or falls down.

It's an old jalopy, said Halftan, and the gas isn't so good.

The world is flat with thick edges. It goes on to a certain point but no further. Then we topple over the edge. We've gone too far already. You say we're heading south, but all the same we're too far north. It's dangerous, mark my words.

Are you afraid, Sergeant?

The edge. Watch out. Don't get too near it. Or . . . or we'll disappear on the bottom side. We'll fall into the stars. Watch out. This can't go on forever.

What will you think of next! You're bored. Here's a little reading matter for you. He handed him a folded slip of yellow paper. Go ahead and read it, there's a flashlight right in front of you. Bachmann took the flashlight which was blacked out except for a tiny spot, and moved the light along the lines. WATCH YOUR STEP, HALFTAN, YOUR HOURS ARE NUMBERED. The warning was written in German. There was no signature, Bachmann turned the note over, found nothing and handed it back to Halftan. That's disgusting. Have you got something on your conscience?

Not that I know of.

Then it's contemptible.

Absolutely contemptible, Sergeant, you're perfectly right.

Take it to the police. That kind of a man has to be punished.

Punished. Yes, that's a fact, but the police are overworked. He'll be punished anyway, don't worry.

If you can lay hands on him. It won't be so easy without a signature or return address.

Never mind, we know where he is.

But can you catch him? People who write threatening letters have sense enough to blow.

Not this one, the best he can do is blow away to heaven. He's dead.

Dead?

That's right. Died of decapitation.

I don't quite understand, Herr Halftan.

It's not difficult, you take a carving knife and cut the head off.

You did that?

Hell, no, a friend did it for five hundred kroner. What people won't do for money! I hired this friend for twenty-four hours, but he's not very reliable, that's why we've got to hurry.

How can a man do such things for money? I can't understand it. He's not a man, he's a—well, a lunatic. He must be. Cutting people's heads off for money, it's barbarous.

Or insane, as you said. His kind can't be convicted.

You don't think so? You think the crime is too awful?

You've got something there. If the crime is too monstrous, no judge can convict—such people are usually declared insane.

I should think so, said Bachmann. He was holding his throat. And it's my sad duty to bring his family the news. Bad, eh? When?

Right now, Sergeant. That's where we're going. The night is young, we've got quite a time ahead of us.

Bachmann dozed. He could neither sleep nor keep his eyes open. He was thinking of the unknown man whose throat Halftan had had cut because of a threatening letter.

Suddenly he heard Halftan's voice: Did you ever see anybody eat paper?

No, who would do a thing like that?

Well, you will see it this evening. The younger brother of the deceased is going to eat the little yellow note I gave you to read.

Another lunatic. What funny people there are nowadays. It's a mad world.

You can say that again, Sergeant Bachmann, a mad world. The parents of the deceased are prominent people. Wait till you hear what they're willing to pay for their dead son.

How much?

What would you think? No, you'll never guess. For the head alone they're going to pay 50,000 kroner. Figure it out. 49,500 clear profit. Not bad, eh?

I still don't get it, said Bachmann.

All right, I'll explain. Halftan lit a fresh cigarette.

The whole thing is political. Everybody in the district thinks I joined the Free Corps to spy for the underground. Nobody knew exactly what was going on until one fine day a certain Frisholm Elshoved, whose head is in a suitcase in the trunk of this car, discovered that this wasn't the case.

Stop, shouted Bachmann. Stop this minute.

Halftan was as frightened as if the Führer in person had bellowed at him. What's wrong?

Stop! I'm burning! Fire!

Halftan bit his lips but jammed on the brakes. Bachmann opened the door and squeezed out of the car.

Where are you going? Halftan shouted. Remember your promise.

It's hot, it's burning hot, Bachmann groaned, took a few steps to the edge of the road, knelt, filled his hands with snow and stuffed the snow into his mouth. He ate at least three handfuls, screaming: hot! hot! and ran back to the car.

Are you thirsty? Halftan asked.

I'm burning, I'm burning. O.K., drive on, but a fire's broken out inside me, haven't you noticed the smoke?

That wasn't smoke, you, you . . . it was warm air.

It looked like smoke.

Yes, that's what it looks like.

Bachmann ate the handfuls of snow he had taken with him and sighed with relief.

It's still smoking, he cried in consternation. Stop. Stop. Again he jumped out of the car, ran to the edge of the road, stuffed his mouth full of snow and ran back.

It's a quarter to eight. Nobody opens his door after eight. If you keep on this way, we'll never get there.

I wasn't invited, Bachmann said, I'm just keeping you company. I can't go back alone now or I would.

No nonsense, Bachmann, you're the only man I can trust. You gave me your word.

The only man. Trust. A man who's as good as his word. There it was again. It sounded like a Te Deum in Cologne Cathedral, like the D-minor chord on the organ.

His head is pretty big too, Bachmann said to himself, and my ears aren't much bigger than his. He looked at Halftan's ear that hung down like a mollusc under the brim of his hat. No, my ears are well shaped. And my head isn't abnormally large. Unfortunately the hair is gone. But there's a hair restorer made out of beeswax.

It's not far from here, said Halftan, it's over there. He pointed at a black speck. I suggest that you simply come in with me, as a friend so to speak. I'll give you my gun. But you won't use it until I tell you. Is that clear? We're friends, that's the best way. No premature decisions. A good general adapts his strategy to the circumstances.

It's cold, said Bachmann suddenly, but it's hot inside. Every time I exhale a cloud of smoke comes out.

It's my cigarette.

No, it's my smoke. Look.

He exhaled: white steam. That's no cigarette. But it's too late.

It's certainly too late to change your mind. Here we are. He gave Bachmann an automatic. It weighed heavy in his hand. Careful, the safety is off. Sergeant, this is a crucial evening for both of us. You have to show what you're worth and I have to prove that I can not only forge plans but also carry them out. You will do what I command, because what I command is necessary. Carry out a monstrous order and despite it all remain a man—that's today's task. Are you ready?

Man, are you ready? The question tortured Bachmann. Readiness is the supreme test. How easy it is to hide in the attic of your own cowardice, to sneak away, to say you're tired, to be sick or get yourself reported sick. How convenient it is to be a brain cell or a grain of dust—when you ought to live, breathe, take risks. To be a man despite it all, that's the crux. Halftan is right about that. Humanity is the most precious of treasures, how true. That magical word rang out like "Silent Night, Holy Night"—sublime and holy. It lifted him out of his doubt, carried him through the night, and plunged his inner conflicts into a tepid bath, into the security of a sanitarium. When the gate closed behind him, the drumming inside Bachmann started up again. Something's wrong. Crazy situation. What can I do all alone in the night with this stranger? This business can end badly. The man's dangerous. You can't trust a man with a red nose. And here I'm carrying his suitcase through a garden. This isn't an army camp. A hotel? I'm tired, dog-tired.

When they came to the house door, he said to himself: now is the time to watch my step. And aloud: I'm a religious man, I don't know what we're planning to do, but it's wrong. It's not pleasing to God. Count me out. I'm a soldier. The last of an old family.

Halftan turned down his collar, beat the snow off his coat, and responded to Bachmann's words with a thin smile. He had him in his power. These people know me, Halftan whispered,

I used to be a teacher. The daughter of the house was my pupil.

He rang. A little bell tinkled far away as though from a sheep lost in the mountains. Nothing stirred. Halftan pulled the bell again. They're home but they're afraid. Can't blame them. He coughed softly. Still nothing stirred.

Bachmann yawned loud and long. This is a hotel and I need sleep. I'm in luck. Four days in the train. Dog-tired. Why don't they open? Helga would have opened long ago. Honnef, Alfred-Rosenberg-Platz 14. Or meet me at the Brown Bear. When I'm not home, I'm at the Bear. She loves me. That time I fell asleep too. It's bad to be tired. You don't dream and you're not awake. Or is it a dream? If I could only sleep, just sleep, and no hurry about waking up.

The door was opened a crack. It was still held by a short chain. Someone said: Herr Halftan? The voice sounded surprised. Then they were both inside.

BARON ELSHOVED AND HIS FAMILY were also hiding from reality. Behind a wall of innocence and clear conscience, they lived in a sanctuary of illusion. Outside the gates the plague had broken out, its name was war, people were dying like flies, mowed down like long grass that had grown too many summers. Promiscuously and with little effort. Or falling as withered autumn foliage falls from the trees, each one a leaf, to make room for a new spring. Good works, piety, and decency were expected to save the Elshoveds from the disaster. They wore their virtues like amulets. In 1944 they lived as in 1844, they had simply forgotten a hundred years. When the Germans came, they did not escape to England. There was no time to make the necessary preparations. They were staunch patriots and a little old-fashioned. Their fear for their private welfare was greater than their hatred of the occupants, and in this respect they were not unlike millions of upright burghers in the occupied territories.

They had managed to hold on to quite a lot. Whole carloads of furniture, china, silver, silk curtains, old paintings in gold frames, jewelry and cash, and a great many liabilities. Only Frisholm, the eldest son, had dared to sally forth from this haven of neutral respectability. He went looking for the plague and its carriers and after some investigation came across the former schoolteacher. Others in the underground movement had also seen through Halftan's double game, but the day of his execution was postponed for various reasons (he was still considered useful). Frisholm's hatred of Halftan dated from his days in grade school when Halftan had tutored him in arithmetic. He burned to pay him back for his mockery and irony. But Halftan had a good memory for each and every one of his former students. Only somebody who has trouble with figures would want to number your hours. He had always detested his students—and the teaching profession. He'd had a whole repertory of nasty punishments for insolent students who tried to undermine his authority.

When the doorbell rang unexpectedly, Thor, Frisholm's younger brother, slipped away to his hiding place under the stairs. His sister Gudrun and his parents preferred to wait in the drawing room. They sent the cook to the door. She had recognized the teacher at once. All sorts of rumors were going around, nobody knew for sure which side this Hjalmar Halftan was on. But when the door closed behind the giant in German uniform, who was carrying a small suitcase in his left hand, she was utterly bewildered. The German's eyes—he was staring into the void as though hypnotized—sent her into an unholy terror. He looked like those wax figures that used to be exhibited at fairs. She trembled and sweated and wiped her hands several times on the knitted woolen jacket she wore over her housedress.

This is a friend, Halftan indicated Bachmann. Don't worry, we won't stay long.

The cook went into the drawing room, closing the door except for a crack. The soldier and his commanding officer stood there like two salesmen. Halftan removed his hat and gloves.

Come in, said the cook. They entered the drawing room. Bjoerk Elshoved, his wife and daughter were seated around the table. They did not stand up, the wood under their fingers gave them a kind of support.

Good evening, said Halftan. We won't stay long.

What is it, Halftan? Bjoerk asked. We weren't expecting you.

I know you weren't expecting me. It's something very important. Concerning your son Frisholm.

What about him? Come to the point.

Is your other son at home?

That doesn't concern you. What is this all about?

I have something to tell you, but I should like Thor to be present.

State your business. Frue Elshoved was even more impatient. We'll tell him later.

I won't speak until you are all together.

Bjoerk stood up: You're wasting your time, speak up or go away.

Thor has to be here first.

To Bachmann the whole conversation seemed weird. He looked around. It was almost like his own home. Old furniture, old pictures, red velvet curtains, thick carpets. The grandfather clock and the Delft china also looked familiar.

The same smell of floor wax, moth balls, perfume, dust and leaves as at home. May I please look at that silver sugar bowl? He pointed to a tea set on a tall cabinet beside him.

Of course. Bjoerk was rather relieved, hoping the German would put it in his pocket.

Bachmann took the sugar bowl in his right hand and seemed to be gauging its weight. Without even looking at it, I can tell it's a Carl Erzmann piece, 1762 or 1764. Carl Erzmann, 1762, said Bjoerk in amazement. I'm a gold- and silversmith, Bachmann explained, in civilian life that is. Carl Erzmann made beautiful things, didn't he?

Yes, yes, definitely. All right Halftan, come to the point.

Bachmann put down the sugar bowl, picked up a milk pitcher and examined it carefully. This too he put down again.

Very well, said Halftan, you don't wish to call your son, though I know he's here. I have news of your second son. He handed Bjoerk the yellow slip. Bjoerk read it without twitching a muscle and passed it on to his wife. Then he pushed the paper back across the table.

Your son wrote that, Baron Elshoved. I remember his handwriting from his schooldays. Don't deny it. It's contemptible, as my friend here remarked earlier in the evening. A man who writes such things is capable of anything.

What do you want? Bjoerk shouted. Are you trying to blackmail me? That's not his handwriting.

Certainly not, said Frue Elshoved.

He wrote it, Halftan repeated.

If you know everything, discussion is superfluous. What do you want?

Seventy-five thousand kroner. Halftan lit his cigarette and tossed the match deftly into the ash tray.

Bjoerk looked at the match, he seemed to be thinking something over: Impossible, Halftan, you haven't earned them.

I'm not asking for any presents, Halftan smiled. I'll give you something in return.

This note? Good-by, Halftan. He stood up. Standing, he was a head taller than Halftan, he might have been fifty-two, with gray, short-cut hair, and the healthy complexion frequent with people who have spent their whole lives in the country. Children and country priests sometimes have that wholesome look.

No, no, not the note. Halftan slowly blew out smoke, I'm selling you the author himself.

I'm not interested. Don't beat about the bush. Have you kidnapped my son, do you want ransom? Those are gangster methods, Halftan, I won't play your game.

So his life is worth nothing to you? Very

You're a gangster, Halftan, get out!

Just one moment. We'll be leaving in a moment. Your living son isn't worth seventy-five thousand to you, good, I'd never have paid that much for the like of him myself. But how much is he worth to you dead? I'll tell you. Exactly two-thirds as much. Fifty thousand kroner.

You're talking nonsense. You bore me.

I beg of you, Herr Halftan, the baroness broke in. We're not as young as we used to be. Go now. Come back another time.

I'm not talking nonsense, sir. A Halftan keeps his promises. Give me the suitcase, Bachmann.

Bachmann handed Halftan the suitcase and opened and closed his left hand, which had gone stiff from carrying it so long.

When the suitcase lay on the table under the lamp, Frue Elshoved and her daughter stood up too and took a short step backward as though the contents might explode.

Just a moment, my honored friends, just a moment. But here we have another guest if I'm not mistaken. Herr Thor Elshoved, no false modesty, this concerns you too. Just step closer. All eyes turned to the far end of the room, which was almost in darkness.

Thor took a few steps. Halftan rested his left hand on the suitcase, with a finger of his right hand he motioned Thor to step closer. Bachmann yawned and rubbed his eyes. The others wore masks of terror. You could hear Thor's shoes on the carpet. He took a few steps and stopped.

The performance can't begin until all are present, step closer, young man. Then Thor stood in the light, a slender, beardless high-school boy in a striped sport shirt.

All eyes turned to Halftan, to his stubby round fingers on the brown leather.

He was the center of attention. The class was as still as a mouse, Halftan was a schoolteacher again. He savored the suspense he had managed to build up.

Ladies and gentlemen, first a brief introduction. I shall try to make myself very clear, and I beg you to listen attentively. It is of the utmost importance to me that there be no misunderstanding between us. In the first place: The rumors that are being spread about me are naive. In the second place: You are in the dark about my activities. In the third place: We are enemies. You belong to a defeated people and I am on the side of the victors. I hope I have made myself clear. And now to the point: I've been in business for almost four years. My merchandise: Information. I buy information and sell it to anyone who can pay. Political information of course. I have a very wealthy employer, who is in a position to pay good, in fact better and better, prices. I'm referring to the Germans. I'm not concerned with ideology, like every good businessman I'm interested in profits. In the last four years I've had a turnover of roughly two hundred thousand kroner. For a poor schoolmaster that's a lot of money. Two years ago I was able, for the first time in my life, to buy something I could never have dreamed of before: A home of my own. Nothing very elaborate, but it's mine, and it has a nice garden. For the first time in my life, I've been able to live like a human being, I can dress, travel, and keep mistresses. I could never afford those things before. I lived like a despicable nobody, from hand to mouth, without prospects, without hope, without a future, without the slightest pleasure. Plenty of people were just as badly off and still are, but that's no excuse for neglecting a personal talent. My talent, and I possess it to the point of genius, is malice. None of us has more than one talent or one life. (Halftan's voice became more passionate.) If somebody you've never molested comes around threatening you with death, that's a serious matter and you've got to take it seriously. You owe it to yourself, especially in these troubled times. If one of your patriots supposes he can save others from death by shooting a German stooge, there's only one possible reply. To act before it's too late. I don't know what you, ladies and gentlemen, would have done in my place, but I know what your ancestors did: If an interloper tried to grab their land and especially if he started threatening the rightful owners, they hired some landless tenant farmer or professional murderer and had the intruder put out of the way. That was the reasonable and right thing to do. It still is. The times haven't changed. The French have a saying: *Plus ça change, plus c'est la même chose.* It was thanks to such ruthless measures that the first Elshoveds acquired their silver and jewelry, their carpets and hangings. The times haven't changed, except in one important point: Today the old landowners are unarmed and defenseless, and the schoolmasters have inherited the earth—a development that could have been foreseen a long time ago.

Here in this little suitcase I have proof that I am perfectly capable of looking out for my own interests. Before showing you the contents, ladies and gentlemen, I wish to request a modest sum in compensation for my business losses. For I have to confess that as of now I am obliged to close up shop. My business is shot, the best I can do is try to save my skin, whether I fall into the hands of the Germans or of the underground, the consequences will be the same. I've decided that it's time for me to pitch my tent somewhere else. 50,000 in cash would come in very handy for my traveling expenses.

This man, a sergeant in the famous Second Hessian Infantry Regiment, will take the money. Incidentally, we're armed, you knew that or I doubt whether you'd have listened to me this long. And one more thing: He's a very good shot. He holds the gold sharpshooter badge. Bachmann, show the ladies and gentlemen your weapon and your badge.

Bachmann was reeling with fatigue. The instant he heard his name, he came wide awake. He pulled out the automatic and aimed it at each in turn. With his left hand he opened his coat, touched his crooked forefinger to the badge and went from one to the other. He also showed it to Halftan.

Splendid, Sergeant, how did you win it?

At Stalino, said Bachmann, I shot twelve Russian monkeys off a roof. He held out the weapon and aimed at the curtain rod. He squeezed the trigger. Everyone jumped. Plaster and dust fell, a dark hole could be seen in the brass rod. Stop that, said Halftan, until I've given the order. But never mind, now our friends know that it's not loaded with candy. Now then, Bjoerk Elshoved, call your cook. Give her the key to the safe or wherever it is you keep your money. I shall count to five. One . . . Aga, Bjoerk cried, Aga. The cook had been standing behind the door since the shot. Yes, please. Pale with terror, she looked from one to the other.

Here's the key, said Bjoerk, giving her three keys on a ring. You know where the box is. Count out fifty thousand and bring them here.

Halftan had set his right foot on a chair, he braced his right elbow on his knee, resting his hand on the suitcase as though the contents might fly away. With his left hand he raised his cigarette to his lips and blew smoke rings under the lamp. Bachmann was still holding the revolver. His eyes were on the silver teapot. Allow me, he said to Bjoerk. He picked it up. No, Bjoerk shouted, I won't allow you.

Bachmann put the teapot down. I'm sorry, he said, but this teapot is really quite magnificent. He bent forward to examine the chasing more closely.

Just as I thought. The two spies returned from the Promised Land, bearing grapes . . . Carl Erzmann has made wonderful fruit bowls too, magnificent pieces. They are a twin set. They're in the Frankfurt museum. Abraham blessing Jacob and Esau, and Joseph and his Brethren. He was especially fond of Biblical themes. Erzmann was a great master. Bachmann smacked his lips. That was great German art. There's nothing like it today.

Rotten times have broken out, he whispered, peace is better. But that's the way it is. The cook came back with several bundles of banknotes. Bachmann stepped aside with a gallant bow to make way for her. She put the money and the keys down in front of Bjoerk. Give Halftan the money. He put the keys in his pocket. She shook her head. I told your mother years ago you'd come to a bad end, Herr Halftan. You've turned into a Wild West gangster.

My poor mother, said Halftan, I could have loaned her some money now. Unfortunately she's not with us any more. May she rest in peace. . . .

The cook wanted to leave the room. Stop! Halftan cried, close the door. You're a member of the household too. Twenty-five years, said the cook.

A long time. That certainly makes you a member. Halftan left the money lying beside the suitcase.

Excellent. And now watch closely, he said. He opened the suitcase, undid the newspaper wrapping and lifted out a young man's head. Picking it up by the hair, he held it under the lamp. The head rotated to all sides. Good, he said. He set the head down beside the suitcase, put in his money and closed it.

That's Frisholm or what's left of him—I hope you're convinced.

Frue Elshoved uttered a loud sigh and fell to the carpet as a stone falls to the ground. Gudrun stood leaning against a wall with wide-open eyes. Thor and his father stood motionless. Only the cook screamed: No! No!

She wanted to run away. No! No! she screamed.

That's not the end yet, said Halftan dryly. The end comes next. We schoolmasters will have a chance only when there's nothing left of you people. Money is only a partial redress, the other part is: Dead people. I need proofs of innocence. Only the dead are innocent and only innocent people deserve to die. Bachmann. The three old people. One bullet each in the head.

Halftan, Bjoerk screamed, he saw the pistol aimed at himself, you're mad.

Wrong, said Halftan, you are. You're defenseless.

Bachmann fired once. He hit Bjoerk in the middle of the forehead. He fired a second time, the cook was standing in profile, he aimed at her temple.

He crossed the room with long steps, pushed Gudrun aside, and put a bullet through the head of the still-fainting Frue Elshoved.

I have two bullets left, said Bachmann.

They won't be needed, Bachmann, not yet. So far so good.

He went up to Thor, who stood paralyzed in the doorway. He took the slip of yellow paper out of his pocket and read: Watch your step, Halftan, your hours are numbered. A morbid joke, the reality is very different. He tore the paper into little pieces. Your bayonet, Halftan. Bachmann yawned and covered his mouth with his right hand, with his left he took his bayonet. Apply it! He indicated a spot on the neck, above the windpipe. Bachmann applied the knife at the spot indicated. The glitter of the steel reminded him of the Carl Erzmann tea set. They made beautiful things in those days, he mused. Nowadays you seldom see such fine work. The candelabrum he had done for his journeyman's examination suddenly struck him as crude. It might have been whittled from wood.

Open your mouth, Thor! Halftan's voice came from far away. Bachmann saw wide-opened eyes and a red throat out of which a tongue grew. The tongue's coated, Bachmann said to himself, that's a sign of fever. He's got three gold fillings, dental gold is worth a lot of money nowadays.

Halftan put the paper into the mouth. Swallow it! he ordered. Thor swallowed, gagged and chewed. In a short while his mouth was empty.

That was fast, Bachmann thought, it would have made me sick to my stomach. How can anybody eat paper?

Halftan tore open Thor's shirt. Thor's chest was white, narrow and hairy. The boy's a stay-at-home, Bachmann thought, so young to be inactive. His father was more powerfully built. Wonder what his brother was built like. You can't tell by the face, not now at any rate. Let me go! Thor roared, let me go!

Cut him open, came Halftan's placid voice. With his left hand Bachmann held the back of Thor's neck and with his right cut him open from throat to abdomen. He had to step aside quickly, for the blood gushed like a spring when the stone is taken away. A man is full of blood, the way a balloon is full of air. It was always fun to burst balloons, it made a bang, it was exciting. A man doesn't make any bang. Thor wheezed and collapsed. The knife had gone through part of the windpipe. Bachmann let him down slowly with his left hand. Wouldn't want the poor kid to fall on his head.

Open the stomach, Halftan commanded. His hands in his coat pockets, he strode back and forth like a general. Bachmann couldn't find the stomach. Halftan pointed. No, that's the liver, the stomach is up here.

Yes, that's right, Bachmann, cut open the stomach. There you are, said Halftan, those little yellow things, he ate the paper just as I predicted.

Thor tried to speak but only a gurgling could be heard. Seen from inside, a man isn't a pleasant sight, people look much better in one piece. What's the fellow gurgling about, I can't understand a word.

Give him a crack, Bachmann, to make him lose consciousness.

Because what's coming now is going to hurt. Bachmann struck Thor in the middle of his forehead with his fist. The gurgling stopped.

Good, well, he won't notice it now, but he's got to have his punishment. Halftan took an earthenware vase from the table, threw out the flowers, and pounded the dying boy with the vase. Bachmann stood tiredly looking on. He was surprised at Halftan's strength. You don't look so strong. I bet you also taught physical education.

Halftan threw away the vase. I should have brought a club. Oh well, that'll do. He gave the dead boy a few kicks. Well, that's that. Halftan straightened up. Physical education? No. But I still swim a good deal. He looked down at Thor: He won't wake up any more, too bad, he's missing the best part.

No, he won't wake up, Bachmann agreed. He's done for.

We're almost finished, Bachmann, there's only the girl left. Gudrun! Halftan roared. She opened wild eyes, her arms were locked over her face. You weren't at the head of your class, frankly, you were hopeless. Well, let's see if there's something else you can do. Take your clothes off! Gudrun stood up and removed her clothes, calmly and without hesitation. She leaned against the wall and smiled.

Are you still innocent, I mean a virgin?

No, said Gudrun in a loud voice.

And you're not afraid? He pointed at Bachmann who stood dozing in the doorway.

No, Herr Halftan. You can have me and he can shoot me or the other way around. She was still smiling. But I'd rather have you, we've known each other longer.

Halftan burst out laughing and just as suddenly fell silent. Good—splendid—marvelous. And what about them?

He pointed at the corpses.

That's what I've always longed for, said Gudrun, her smile was like a mask over her lips, I've dreamed of it often. And now it's come true.

Halftan couldn't understand. She must be out of her mind, he said to himself.

Not once, a hundred times I've dreamed it just like this, Gudrun repeated. I didn't love my family. If you'd known them better.

Halftan smiled too, incredulous, she's trying to put one over on me. She's tricky. Do you mean that?

I mean it all right, Gudrun nodded, I certainly do. I can only thank you, Herr Halftan.

Halftan felt cold, a shudder ran through him, he looked across at Bachmann, who had fallen asleep on his feet. His lower lip drooped. He twitched a few times in his sleep, made faces, snored through his nose, cleared his throat and went on sleeping. Halftan went over to him, took the automatic out of his pocket, checked the two cartridges in the magazine, put on the safety catch and slipped it into his pocket. Bachmann slipped slowly to the floor, belched none too gently, but went on sleeping. His head hung down sideways.

Gudrun stood motionless, leaning forward in an attitude of invitation. When Halftan approached her, she laid a thin hand on his arm. For a moment he looked at her penetratingly, then brushed her hand off. His desire had passed. She doesn't seem to mind, she doesn't scream and struggle, on the contrary, she wants to have an orgy with her dead parents and brothers looking on. He was disgusted. He'd imagined a very different scene, he'd expected an outburst, wild hysterical screams. And here she was perfectly calm. That took the wind out of his sails. The little pink nipples of her young breasts didn't tempt him, they looked to him like a puppy's teats, her little bit of pubic hair was neither exciting nor inviting—he was disappointed. The sleeping Bachmann, the corpses, it all made him smile. Funny, he said, funny.

Gudrun didn't take her eyes off him. When their glances met, she too smiled. He felt a complicity with her, a forgiveness and understanding that he hadn't asked for but that he was willing to accept if they were offered. Of course she's insane, he repeated to himself. The shock has driven her mad.

Put your clothes on, I've changed my mind. As he watched her dressing, he remembered: nine years ago she was still in my class. Her short blond pigtails, her lively blue eyes, her snippety rejoinders and the proud, self-reliant way she walked and talked. A hundred times I thought of taking her, by cajolery, by force . . . and now that there's nothing more to fear, neither parents nor brothers, now that I could kill her, I don't want her any more.

It was time to be going. The room smelled putrid. He shook Bachmann awake. Bachmann opened his eyes, stared at the girl putting her clothes on, saw a strange but familiar man in a gray overcoat, with his hat pushed back rakishly on the back of his head. He looked around. A head was growing out of the table top, as if the man had forced his way through the wood and died of exhaustion. Bodies were lying around, probably dead, under the table and in among upset chairs. Flowers on the floor and not far away, in a little pool of blood, a vase. There were wet spots on the gray carpet, some pink, some black, as if wine had been spilled, wine out of flower vases. Someone dropped it. Wetness, mud. He wasn't going to try it, but he knew: If you step on one of those spots, you'll sink. They're deeper than you think, the floor boards are soaked, you'll fall through to the foundations of the house. Bottomless mud. The same as then. They were standing a minute ago, and now all of a sudden they're lying there. One chewing, another talking, and now they're lying still. They all sank in, and anybody who stuck out was ripped to pieces by iron splinters.

Bachmann stood up. Voroshenko—it's just like then. I've seen this before, he said.

Good, said Halftan. Stop gaping then. We're leaving. He took the suitcase and opened the door for Gudrun. He followed her, took a coat from the clothes rack and hung it over her shoulders. He also found a fur cap and handed it to her. Bachmann's eyes passed over the bodies and the disorder; they stopped on the Carl Erzmann tea set. The silver had a subdued sheen. The two spies from the Promised Land carrying grapes on a pole. The grapes were like waves, the spies strode forward feather-light. He'd have liked to take the teapot, nobody'll miss it now. It's really lovely, exquisite. And now they'll be walking on alone, and nobody'll see them. He grew sad. But good upbringing is stronger than greed. He closed the door softly so as not to wake anyone. Again he felt emptiness and disappointment as five days before when forced to leave Göritz's battalion. Again the world was dead. Everything repeats itself, how strange, isn't there anything new? On the entrance posts at the end of the path two little snow-covered stone lions sat like sentries. Sat on their haunches with open eyes, peering silently out into the night. As he passed, he bent one knee and crossed himself. Here we sit, the two of us, Halftan and I, we've turned to stone animals. Covered with snow.

As THE ROAD INTO THE MOUNTAINS grew steeper, he saw on one side the jagged lines of high woods, black against a black sky. On Halftan's side the mountain fell away steeply, the great dark surface was untouched. The woods came toward them and suddenly they were driving through a lane of tree trunks, a kind of double wall from which there seemed to be no escape. The wall seemed never to end and Bachmann was afraid that the road would suddenly stop and there'd be a lake six thousand feet below. He was wide awake like someone who has recovered from his fatigue at three in the morning and can't fall asleep again. The creaking of the wheels pained him. The silence inside the car was like an echo dying away. Only breathing could be heard. On the back seat, under a blanket, lay Gudrun, maybe she was asleep, at any rate she didn't stir. And now, Bachmann, said Halftan out of a clear sky, let's draw up the balance sheet. The whole operation took thirty-five minutes, or including the preparatory phase, seven hours. That makes more than seven thousand kroner an hour, expenses deducted. We've accomplished a good deal and lost nothing. We made one mistake. We should have taken the jewelry. I weighed the pros and cons and decided the jewels might attract attention in case we were stopped by a patrol. It didn't occur to me that this girl in the back seat could have worn them. Now it's too late, everything went off smoothly, we were in luck. Especially you, Herr Bachmann, though you didn't know it. (He took two automatics from his pocket.) You see, I always carry a second weapon, if you had refused, you'd be dead now. That's how it is, Sergeant. If you have your senses, you live, if you haven't you die. What better proof that you've got your precious reason, whatever the medical board may think! Instinctively you've always done the right thing, you probably did in Voroshenko or whatever you call it, and now again today. What more do you want?

Where are you taking me? I've got to sleep.

Not to Narvik, that would be awkward. Your regiment is south of Narvik now, on the same railroad line.

What regiment? What are you talking about?

Didn't you want to join your regiment or some special duty battalion. Or did I misunderstand you?

There's no hurry about that now, Herr Halftan.

I can see you're getting more sense by the minute. I've said so all along, and sooner or later your reason will get its official recognition. Because you only believe what you see in black and white, am I right?

I wanted, Bachmann stammered, I wanted to prove that I'm not afraid of anything. I've killed four people without batting an eyelash and without losing my reason—that was good and it was necessary. No, I didn't lose control of myself, I wasn't upset, I kept cool. That's the main thing. But the moment I left the house it started up. Bachmann ran his hand over his face as though to warm it or to make sure he was still alive. Something started up, I don't know what, but when I closed the door behind me, I had a vision.

Are you making up stories again, Bachmann?

No, no. He seemed to be talking in his sleep, no, you can't tell me any different. I saw something, but I can't talk about it yet.

What we've just done, Herr Bachmann, is something I've always wanted to do, it was an old dream. In peacetime I never got the chance, but then with the war the chance suddenly came. All by itself. That's the good thing about war. You come to yourself. You mustn't be afraid of people, my friend, people are only flesh.

Where are you taking me, Herr Halftan?

To the front, Halftan laughed, you're a crack shot. You've done first-class work. If I could afford it, I'd hire you for a few years. But the war won't last that long and in peacetime you won't be worth a nickel. You'll be like everybody else. A respectable citizen.

The road went downhill, they were driving very fast, and unexpectedly the wall of tree trunks stopped. The weather had changed, the sky was clear but moonless. Scattered through the whiteness were the dispersed roofs of solitary farms, here a tree, there a small clump of trees. Cattle barns floating like driftwood in the sea. And always the curved lines of the hills, the broken line of treetops, a monotonous repetition of rising and falling lines. Landscape, nature, had only one effect on Bachmann, to make him sad. He wanted to blot it out, to do away with everything that seemed dead but wasn't really dead, perhaps because he felt cheated. To smooth out all those wavy lines with his hand, to push aside the stars outside the windows and clear a path through them. He'd have liked to scratch the snow off the mountains with both hands and pile it up somewhere else, or sweep it into the sea. Just sweep it away, into the water with it! He'd have gladly ripped up every single birch by the roots, tied it up like a bouquet and put it in a vase. He hated nature from the bottom of his heart, never had he hated it so passionately. He had always detested nature, even as a child he had avoided hikes and outings, with the years his strange fear of nature and his hatred of everything green had increased. That night after leaving his battlefield his very bones ached with hatred. He closed his eyes and instantly saw the one thing in nature that he loved: a Christmas tree. Candles and tinsel, glittering silver threads and gold stars, colored globes and sweets put him in a merry mood. What do you want to be when you grow up, his hunchbacked Aunt Klärchen asked. She repeats the question and he repeats his answer because it contributes to the general merriment: Salta Claus, said the four-and-a-half-year-old Gauthier, who already looked like a twelve-year-old. I'd like to be a Salta Claus. (His N's were never quite right, he simply can't pronounce an N and always says L.) You could put on a beard right now, and his tiny aunt picks him up on her lap, completely disappearing beneath the child, and everybody bursts out laughing, snorting, coughing. You're big enough. Lot yet, Bachmann hears himself saying. He smiled. Lot yet, lot yet, he cried aloud.

What's that?

Nothing, nothing, I used to have trouble with my N's. I couldn't pronounce them and I wanted to be a Santa Claus. Maybe you missed your calling, but your business isn't so bad. Who wouldn't be happy to spend his whole life with jewels, gold, and silver?

I'm a gold- and silversmith, Herr Halftan, those are my materials, of course I like them, but there is a limit to everything. Let's not talk about it. All of a sudden I wish there were peace, that this war were over, then I could start all over again. I still have my master examination ahead of me.

Just the same I should have taken them, Halftan sighed, that was a mistake. Then he suddenly threw on the brakes and got out.

Bachmann wanted to stretch his legs and got out too.

Don't you want to get out? Halftan called into the car. Gudrun didn't stir. She's asleep, he said, thank God she's still alive. What I'm going to do with her I don't know yet, I'll think of something. I'd have liked to take her with me.

Take her with you, where to?

I don't know that yet either. So far everything has been simple. Now it's getting more complicated, Herr Bachmann. Somewhere on a branch a hundred swallows are sitting, their nests are woven of silver wire, instead of eggs they have diamonds. But they don't hatch them, they sit on a tree nearby, waiting to see what will happen. But nothing happens, nothing will ever crawl out of those glittering eggs. They will neither live nor lose their sparkle. The sky is a dirty brown, the sun lies low, like a lost coin in the fields. And suddenly it's noon, a dazzling stroke of lightning, a magnesium flare. In one second every living creature is extinguished, everything dissolves into white powder. But my swallows are still sitting black on the branches, waiting for shells to burst open where there are no shells and for chicks that don't exist to crawl out. The swallows are porcelain. The tree was painted on the street with tar. That's why. Now do you understand? I wrote it all down twelve years ago, word for word. And now it comes back to me. Do you understand me now?

Not a word, said Bachmann, but very much against my will I still like you.

Halftan grew angry: Forget it, I haven't said anything.

There wasn't much to be seen, the stars had paled, but one could sense the broad unobstructed land and a sky that seemed to drop down into the insides of the earth. They were over a valley. Halftan stood twenty paces from the car, he had pushed his hat forward and was urinating. He pressed his hands to his sides as though standing beside an open grave, sunk in devotion. Suddenly he shook himself like a dog coming out of the water and went to the car. He raised the hood and checked the water in the radiator. The need to urinate, contagious as everyone knows, spread to Bachmann. The giant's figure was a monument. Solitary and firm he stood there like a statue of Christ in the Italian Alps. With birdie in hand, he looked up at the stars. Eternity, eternity, said a Nietzschean murmur within him, how big you are! O starlight that floods the cosmos (his arc grew shorter and shorter)! Heaven and earth, clouds and space! said

Bachmann aloud. Not so loud! Halftan called. Earth and heaven, I belong to you! Bachmann added emphatically. The stream gave out, he shook the last drops from his member, but forgot to put it away. He took a few steps as though looking for a good place to take a run for a leap to the moon. Leaning against the open hood of the car, a cigarette in the corner of his mouth, Halftan was watching him. That's a fine case of madness. He was impressed by the German giant, striding through the snow with his penis in hand.

He loved the Germans and they fascinated him. As a Norwegian he felt insignificant, provincial, and inferior beside them. Everything impressed him about Bachmann, even his shadow, even the way he could reel off poems by Nietzsche. He envied him as if it had always been his most fervent wish to be Gauthier Bachmann. His only consolation was the certainty of his own genius, whereas the other was an overgrown fool. And another thing troubled Halftan: his own fear of God. It's safe to assume that the fear of God has never touched him, he's an antediluvian monster, beyond good and evil, zoologically a new continent, *Homo bachmannus.* The idea appealed to him. What is *Homo bachmannus?* He has the body of a horse, the intelligence of a chimpanzee, and the soul of a dove. Halftan congratulated himself on his definition. Naturally this species survived the deluge, it will never be extinct. The whole world is crawling with them, he must have been some freak in the ark.

If you don't put it away pretty soon, it's going to freeze up, Halftan laughed, that happens up here. Bachmann buttoned his fly. Yes, Herr Halftan, he said, still in a dream, eternity is large. The world is wide and the heavens are endless. We've got to hold on to our reason. Mustn't let ourselves be carried away, man is so insignificant (Bachmann pointed down into the valley) compared to all that.

No comparison, Halftan muttered. Naturally there's no comparison. He closed the hood. We've got to be going. The night won't last forever.

They got in. The bundle in the back seat still made no move. Lovely creature, said Halftan, wanted to seduce me. Horrible. Do you believe in God, Bachmann?

Yes, I was brought up that way.

I'm not asking how you were brought up but whether you believe in Him.

Yes and no, I'm not sure. On the one hand yes—but on the other hand no. Exactly as Halftan had expected. That means you don't believe, he said. Fundamentally you don't give a shit.

Bachmann didn't like to be regarded as an atheist, for atheist always smacks of socialist. No, I wouldn't say that. I just have my doubts, like everyone else.

Halftan was firm. It means you don't believe. A man like you can't afford to have doubts. You're too delicately put together. The soul of a dove. That's right. He opened the window and spat out. After what's happened this evening it's perfectly plain. You're too weak to believe in God. You're too weak period. Weak and delicate as a child. The kid back there is stronger than you.

Me? A child? That's a good one. Bachmann laughed with frank incredulity.

I believe in God and fear Him, and for that reason I fear no man. That's why I can give orders and you have to obey. That's why I don't have to soil my hands. He cleared his throat angrily. Phooey, Bachmann, you're a monster.

Bachmann felt sick. You seduced me.

Only a child lets himself be seduced. I used you. As an alibi. Nobody around here would think a plain soldier capable of such things. They think such things are only done by the SS or the Quislings.

Bachmann stared straight ahead. Halftan's words cut into his heart like a bayonet—though they drew less blood. The snow-covered hills danced before his eyes. The stars broke down into colors and patterns and returned to their former state. I must be insane. Maybe they were right.

You're very crafty, Herr Halftan, I can see that.

You're not the least bit mad, you're perfectly reasonable. You're a reasonable man. You kept your promise. You said yourself that you felt better. It's intelligent to do what helps you. The board of appeal will decide in your favor. You'll see. Unfortunately you haven't entirely surmounted fear, but that too is human. Everybody has fears. Call it madness. Everybody who doubts God is afraid to die and afraid not to die. And most of all afraid of guilt and punishment. Call it conscience.

But those people were innocent, Bachmann groaned.

That's absurd. In a war nobody's innocent. Or everybody. Innocence is an obsolete concept. Nowadays you're either for one side or the other. Active or passive. Nobody's innocent.

You betray and murder your own people.

Only betray, others do the murdering for me. It took me a long time to find out how simple and cheap it is. I may be an evil genius, but in any case I'm a genius. I used to be an under-paid schoolteacher and a socialist. When the Germans came, my eyes opened. And how did they come? They took us by surprise. Because they knew we were defenseless. It wasn't Herr Quisling but our weakness that lost us our independence. Quisling's treason is a legend, the truth is that we were unable to defend ourselves. What's good enough for the German Army is good enough for me. I learned my lesson, I haven't done so badly in the last four years. There are lots of pious people in this country, they talk all kinds of nonsense, anybody who listens to them is sunk. They say for instance: The spirit is stronger than the flesh. God's justice will conquer. Brute force will melt away like snow in the spring. That's mental derangement, pure Nordic hogwash. The spirit is made of armor plate and gunpowder, spirit is brute force, and without brute force there's no spirit. A democracy that can't defend itself is a figment of the brain.

Voroshenko, the mud, seven hundred and sixty-three in three hours, Bachmann whimpered.

And fear, Halftan broke in.

One minute they're standing on their feet and the next they're gone.

So what! It's all fear.

But fear is human, I don't understand.

That's why you're human too, why you have the soiled hands and not I. Everything is human, especially wars, and those people this evening were simply victims of war.

But they were innocent. Bachmann's hands were perspiring.

I've explained that. Everyone is innocent and no one, I'm not the only one to profit. The underground will call it a provocation, it will reinforce their resistance. As far as our side is concerned, those people were potential enemies, there won't be any fuss—only I, personally, am through.

Bachmann gaped as though seeing ghosts. He saw a hundred faces and they were all lying with their mouths open on tables, in the grass, on footpaths. They lay as lifeless as dead trees, their branches splintered by shells, and instead of blood, swamp water overflowed the gutters, formed puddles, spilled over, ran into the railroad station, into the men's toilet and down on the tracks. On the platform it froze into ice. And a sharp face with a lieutenant's insignia under it stuck out of the ice and said: You're insane. Nerves of steel. We have to do violence to nature. A second later he was lying in the mud of Voroshenko that was swallowing up the whole army, he opened his fly and furiously jabbed his member into the mud.

Whore, came a screaming voice, I'm going to fuck you to

death. Till you break open and fall apart. Then I'll crawl inside and up. I'll explode you from inside. Up and down went his member, caressed by moisture and warmth. But it struck nothing. A door was barricaded, but he didn't get in that far. Darling, darling, the voice moaned, and then a hissing and sliding as of stones falling into a pond, a gushing and pounding as of water being poured over his head from boots and filling his ears and nostrils. The water ran between trees, they were as short as table legs, and made spots. More power, more force. The armor plate must burst and break and at last I'll be inside. He lay deep below the roots of the trees, from which grew polished branches, and his mouth was full of black earth. Suffocating, he sat up and shouted at Halftan: I should have killed you!

I'm no judge of that. Halftan threw away his cigarette and opened his collar. There were frost blossoms on the windows, but inside the car it was hot.

From the back seat came a thin voice:

Herr Halftan, I'm hungry. When do we eat?

Halftan reached into his pocket, found a piece of chocolate and handed it back.

I don't know if we'll eat today, but we'll make up for it tomorrow. Eat the chocolate and think about something else.

I've been trying to the whole time, but I can't think of anything else. I want a big juicy steak and potatoes and asparagus and first soup and then fresh fruit and cheese. I'm hungry.

Don't be a baby.

Then I want a warm luxurious hotel room with a bath, a big marble bathtub, and soak two hours until I'm all sweet and luscious. And then you come in or the two of you until it kills me, it must be so wonderful. But maybe I don't want to die, and it doesn't have to be so wonderful, but I want to tremble and dissolve. I want you to bite my neck, you belong to me, only to me, but he belongs to me too, I want you to make me bleed to death, but without pain. No, maybe not to death.

Quiet, said Halftan, quiet. We'll eat tomorrow, and now think about something else. And you just think of killing, he said to Bachmann. Bachmann turned around to him. This stranger's face looked more and more familiar to him, as if he'd seen it somewhere. He liked him better than ever.

What made you do it, Herr Halftan? Tell me the reasons.

Reasons? First, I enjoyed it; if you insist, I'd always wanted to do something like that. In the second place, money isn't to be sneezed at, in the third place we were political enemies. What do you need reasons for? That's your business. You don't have to answer. And one more thing. If I were a coward and had to prove my courage, I wouldn't have done it that way. But I'm not afraid, only of God. He and I are close relations. We're above sins and virtues. But you're a human, or something of the sort.

Lizards, said Bachmann dully, I see lizards in every hole. Each man for himself, each against all. And everywhere death.

Everywhere death—that may be. But you forget one thing—in between there are sun and flies, amusements and lots of hunting.

Bachmann said nothing for a time, he looked out into the darkness and tried to concentrate. Only this afternoon I was with that young lieutenant, what was his name, oh yes, Hupfenkar, stupid name and so young, then a bus came and some fifty soldiers got in, they were all in high spirits, maybe they were going to some celebration. The bus drove off and I was still sitting there like a schoolboy who's missed his trip to the country—and this young whippersnapper lectures me. He says I shouldn't talk so much—I should be glad, that's what everybody's been telling me—I should thank my stars. They all hate being soldiers. That's a funny thing, I don't. They're all together, they have comradeship, and I'm alone. They laugh together, die together—and I'm still alone. And then this character comes around and says he needs me. Admires me, says I'm his man. Doesn't even realize I'm a donkey. An idiot who's ashamed to be the son of a Bachmann. What does he know anyway, he doesn't know my people. We're an old, respected family, there are Bachmanns in every district council and school board. We even have a bishop in the family. What does he know? A schoolteacher without any family background, intelligent maybe, but no tradition behind him. An insignificant nobody. And the likes of him challenges me. As if he knew I had something out of kilter. I was never a hard man, I only looked that way. Because I'm so big. Can I help it? None of my ancestors was squeamish. They all got ahead in the world. If they'd all had an uneasy conscience like me—what would have become of us? Only those who have nothing to lose can afford to be respectable citizens and cowards. Halftan knew that.

His ancestors cramped him or was it the small car? He tried to stretch but collided in all directions. He lowered his head, took off his cap and spoke like a lamb to its shepherd:

Cornelius Beekman, the founder of our family, had to poison his predecessors before he could become guild master in Ghent. His sons Frederik and Janus, who fled from the Reformation, wouldn't have been given the right of asylum in Cologne if they'd refused to spy on the other Flemings. As late as 1840 a Bachmann, a great-granduncle, had to burn down the house of a goldsmith because the man was discrediting the whole guild by selling gold spoons made out of some tin alloy. And to tell you the whole truth, fate didn't even spare my own father. He was sorely tried too. Just imagine, a respected citizen, master of the guild and town councilor, and by government order he had to deliver counterfeit articles. To the day of his death he never forgave himself. He was all broken up, it had a good deal to do with his illness.

He felt more and more uncomfortable. His father snarled out of his grave: Shut up, you Santa Claus, but Bachmann couldn't stop: The alloy crumbles when I use it, the metal has lost its sheen and hardness. I've never mentioned it to anyone, but I'm telling you.

Good, said Halftan. That's fine. The humble voice of the giant, who came of such a fine family, whose members had been swine for generations, cheered him up. The irony of fate—those people he killed today might have been his relatives. That gave him double pleasure. Wolf eat wolf, he gloated. That's a good one. The old socialist of the twenties cropped up in Halftan.

Gudrun's voice cried out from the rear: I'm hungry—I'm starving.

Be still! Halftan shouted. It's just getting interesting. A man made of gold is disintegrating into scraps of paper. Side by side with the class fighter, Halftan had within him a gold digger, and still deeper down a man in love with gold and jewelry. A real enthusiast—who worshiped jewels like a God and God like a jewel.

Bachmann went on undeterred—for confession was good for him whom true faith had almost forsaken. It cleansed him like an enema: deep within, under the gold, the iron is rusting. Air and water have seeped in and are corroding it. It's crumbling, soon it will all dissolve into air. Gold will turn to dirt and dirt to muck. Soft, deep, smelly muck. Phooey—I make myself sick. I can smell myself.

Good, said Halftan again, that's interesting.

It can't go on like this, Herr Halftan. What would become of me? Something has to happen or I'll rot. Something to make me as hard as steel. Hard, hard. He repeated the word several times and gnashed his teeth. To be hard—that's the only solution. Cool, always guided by reason. That's the only way. I know it. But it's so difficult. Never to lose your reason, always to remain your plain self.

He sighed, passed his hands over the thin hair that grew out of his skull like yellow down and was now sticking to his scalp. He put his cap back on.

He had nothing more to confess.

We're almost there, Halftan announced, it won't be long now. Then you can go back where you came from.

I'm going to Honnef, said Bachmann with a look of happiness. I've got a girl. She sings like a nightingale, that's what they call her. She's almost as big as I am. She doesn't know how much I love her.

So you see, Bachmann, life isn't so dreary after all. Suddenly Halftan burst out laughing and surveyed this German phenomenon. Bachmann joined in the laughter.

I say shoot and you shoot, Halftan laughed. I say cut him open and you cut the poor kid open. I say knock him out and you pretty near kill him. He doubled up with laughter. You're quite a number. You've really let yourself be made an ass of, ha—ha—ha! He blew his nose and wiped away the tears. Lord, what lunatics there are in the world today! And all that for a few compliments. With one hand he lowered the window and opened the suitcase with his other, took a handful of banknotes and threw them out. The paper fluttered outside the window and fell into the snow or blew away.

Paper, nothing but paper, Halftan laughed, absolutely worthless. You can't buy a thing for it (he let the bills run through his fingers, then he picked up the suitcase in one hand, shook the rest out the window, knocked the suitcase against the car door and threw it away).

That's that, he said. That ought to show you that money means nothing to me, nothing at all.

Suddenly he stepped on the brake as if he'd come to a barrier on the road and jumped out.

Herr Halftan, Gudrun cried, don't leave me alone. Bachmann got out too, he wanted to see what there was to stop for. Halftan ran fifty paces into a field, the snow wasn't very deep.

When Gudrun saw she was alone in the car, she was afraid. She threw off the blanket and ran after Halftan. Don't leave me alone, I'm afraid.

First Bachmann wanted to run after them, then he changed his mind. Throwing all his money away, he's gone mad.

He saw Halftan dropping to his knees, perhaps fifty paces from the road. He heard him screaming: O great radiant God, You're not in heaven but standing right here above me. You glitter as never before—You've put on all Your jewels for me. Come lower, lower.

Halftan bent down and shouted "lower—lower." He stretched out his arm and clenched his fist. Now I've got You. Come here, Gudrun, here. Gudrun was already standing behind him like a shadow. Bend down, bend down—here beside me. Gudrun dropped to her knees. Halftan pulled her down. He won't stay long, Gudrun. He can leave any minute. Let's shoo Him away, and see if we can do it again. Suddenly he was holding an automatic, he pressed it to Gudrun's temple and fired.

Nothing has happened, came an astonished voice, a bang and it's all over. But He is still here. He crawled on his knees to another place, holding the automatic in his right hand. Let's try again—maybe it'll work this time. Another report. Halftan fell forward.

What's he done this time?

Bachmann decided to take a look. He lifted Halftan up.

Something that looked like black water was running down his right cheek. He was dead.

Bachmann went to the car, shrugged his shoulders and looked for the gear shift. He found cigarettes, sniffed at them and threw them out the window. He stepped on the gas, after a mile or so the road began to slope down and he saw the lights of a village. The first road signs and a little further on plates with street names. The road kept going downhill. Behind him the sky grew lighter. He smelled the sea. Gray stripes settled like wisps of smoke on the roofs. In Bachmann too a light dawned as all alone he steered the unfamiliar car through narrow streets. My obstinacy is madness, he thought. It was all wrong. I'm a fool. I ought to be glad to be getting out of uniform, instead I'm fighting to keep it on. Helga. I'll take her to Duisburg and introduce her to my mother. Won't she be surprised! Nobody ever thought I was capable of getting married. Marriage. Daily obligations. Children. Everything in its proper place. Order. And friends. And a profession. Once I've passed the master examination they can all kiss my. They'll be amazed—they never expected it.

In the middle of his daydreams he remembered the board of appeal. Helga had brought her connections to bear. Now I'll have to go. She's fixed everything up for me. She knows everybody. I can't let her down. I've got to go. But I'll put on some act. I'll tell them every detail. If they don't doubt my sanity then, they've got a screw loose themselves. But if the police ask about me, then, well, I'll tell them I acted under hypnosis—anyway, I was on sick leave. Bachmann smiled. I'll stay sick. Until further notice. Sickness is the best way. After all, I am mentally deranged. He laughed. I'll be discharged. Hurrah! Let other people risk their necks. I'm a free man.

Clarity was born in Bachmann, the daylight helped. There was only one thing left behind:

Yes, that's bad, he said to himself, that's bad. Killed four people. That's no good. If they'd only been armed, it wouldn't have happened, Halftan wasn't entirely wrong. So now I'm supposed to take the fear and cowardice of the victims upon myself? Nothing doing. Better not think about it. That's the best way.

In sight of the station, Bachmann stopped the car. He got out, took his knapsack, adjusted his cap and approached. A sign said SOERSUND in big letters. For a few moments he stood undecided in the snow. Then he went in and found a heated waiting room. No one had to show him the way, he just followed the snoring. In the waiting room soldiers and girls, civilians and children were lying side by side and crisscross. But not far from the stove he found a square yard of vacant floor. He laid his head on his knapsack and fell asleep immediately.

Outside, day came and the first gulls swooped down. At the end of Platform One a drunken sailor was clutching the handle to the toilet door with one hand and trying to get a hold on the air with the other. He vomited. A clanking of metal was heard. A whistling and hissing. A few hundred yards below the station cars were being shunted about. The first English bombers flew in from the sea.

After vain gropings in the air the sailor lost his grip and fell. His head stuck out over the loading platform.

III

WHERE ARE YOU GOING, Helga?

To the Brown Bear.

Helga.

Yes, Frau Doktor.

I gave you the attic room under one condition.

And now you want to get paid, I never expected any different (Helga thinks).

Helga, I've been putting up with this long enough.

You are one to talk. (Helga thinks).

We have our house rules.

I haven't done anything, Helga risked.

You haven't done anything? This can't go on.

What's wrong?

Two days ago I find a midget in the garbage can. Said he was your illegitimate child.

I don't know any midgets.

Two weeks ago a legless soldier on the stairs, acting as if the whole house belonged to him. Whistling and singing at three o'clock in the morning. That was enough for me. I need the room next week.

And what do you expect me to do?

I don't know. We were all young once, but there are limits. You belong in the Bear, not in my house. Frau Doktor Gram closed the door behind her, the scent of sweet roses filled the vestibule.

ON TUESDAY NIGHT AS ON EVERY OTHER NIGHT, there was dancing at the Brown Bear. In the Bear infantrymen, schoolgirls, foreign forced laborers, whores, sailors and salesgirls found what they could find nowhere else. Mirko Janko's Bulgarian Band and plenty of atmosphere. Neither the Father Rhine nor the Green Huntsman could compete with the Bear, for in the Bear the benches were placed in discreet niches and the tables were so low that no one could see what was going on underneath. The Bear was also patronized by retired gentlemen who wanted to be young. The Brown Bear wasn't a wild place, even if the goings on were wild and woolly seven nights a week. Actually the Brown Bear was Mirko Janko and his Gypsies, and without Janko it would have been a dreary small-town bar. Janko and his Gypsies fiddled and trumpeted louder than a Krupp cannon, better than the S.A. Band, and with more gusto than the Bad Honnef Municipal Orchestra. Janko and his associates left infantrymen winded and German maidens with aching feet, so making a modest contribution to the cause of the partisans in far-off Bulgaria. When Mirko announced a new number, it always sounded like SMRT FASCISTU (Death to the Fascists). But even if there had been any Fascists in the Bear, and there weren't, they wouldn't have understood his language. For it also sounded like STARS OF HOME. Stars of Home was a good song, for every one of the guests was at home somewhere outside of town (if only in the next village), and each one of them, whether German or foreigner, was left with an emotional experience. That marvelous, inimitable hospital-ward-on-Christmas-Eve feeling of brotherhood, the feeling of universal, almost cosmic unity which sometimes, all too seldom, alas, comes over all men.

That Tuesday night Mirko was in especially high spirits, for Helga (she had no way of knowing that Bachmann, her boy friend, would suddenly turn up) had promised him the night. For this one night Mirko had done various things that went against his nature. For two months he had let Helga sing every evening, though he detested her tremolos. Now at last the time had come. Mirko was playing like a madman and the Bear's temperature had reached the boiling point when the request program began with YOU ARE THE FAIREST.

> You are the fairest woman on the continent
> Hello (some shouted Sieg Heil)
> even if I haven't a red cent
> you've given me a bed
> Hello (some shouted Sieg Heil)
> And here I'll rest my head
> Hello hello
> until you quench my fire
> and I still your desire.
> Hello hello hello.

The number had to be repeated, it was very popular. During the applause an elderly gentleman passed out.

Mirko stepped up to the mike, stroked his mustache with his index finger and smiled broadly. His gold and silver teeth sparkled.

Ladies and gentlemen. In response to a general request we are again presenting THE SWALLOWS. (Bravo, bravo!) It also gives me pleasure to announce that after much urging Fräulein Helga Okolek has finally agreed to sing this beautiful song from her Bavarian homeland. (Helga, Helga!) The entrancing, the charming nightingale of Honnef, Fräulein (music) Helga (louder music) Okolek (still louder music), here she is! Surprise, coughing, but no Helga. Just one moment please. Janko found Helga in the farthermost corner of the room, where those who came in directly from work tucked themselves away. She hadn't heard Janko approaching. Gently wagging her head, she was looking into Bachmann's light-blue eyes, holding his left hand in both of hers. Bachmann was sipping at his beer, which he held in his right hand, it was he who had first seen Janko, who stood there speechless. Janko swallowed his jealousy: Helga, do I have to send you an invitation?

Without turning around, Helga said: No, I'm coming. She squeezed Bachmann's hand, stood up and followed Janko.

Forgive the delay, said Janko into the mike, a slight technical difficulty. His voice sounded edgy, and he wasn't laughing any more. When Helga seized the microphone in both hands, a storm roared through the Bear as if the Führer had appeared in person, and then the room was perfectly still. For those who had never seen Helga the experience was unprecedented. Before their eyes stood a Valkyrie in a short blue dress, disclosing stout calves and powerful knees that gave promise of heavenly thighs. She towered over all the musicians. Her breasts were bigger than the legendary blue mountains and just as unlikely, her bottom was as round as a terrestrial globe. She had black waved hair and unpainted red cheeks. Everything about Helga was big, her eyes, her mouth, her nose, and her ears, as if she had developed from double instead of single cells. She smiled and said in a pleasant voice: This evening I am going to sing a song from my Bavarian homeland, THE SWALLOWS (a few Bavarians shouted: Grüss Dich. Juchhe!). The applause was stupendous:

I'm only a little swallow,
far away from my nest,
looking for my food

where I can find it best.
The winter has gone by,
and spring is in the air,
but I alas am caught
in your beloved snare

Even after this first verse the applause was deafening. Skinny
Maria, as much a part of the place as the glasses, was sobbing
loudly. Helga's big brown eyes glistened. Towering over the
entire audience, she looked across the room to her lover, who
responded by lifting his glass. Bachmann felt as if he was
sitting in an aquarium. Seaweed, sea horses and colored fishes
were floating through the room and forming clusters. The
biggest and bluest of them opened its mouth. Either it'll swallow
them all, or they'll rush it and bite it to death. He felt the
tension mounting as the blue, giant fish opened and closed its
mouth in secret fish language. Something's going on in here,
they're cooking up some kind of plot, there's blood lust in their
eyes, their teeth are sharp, they have weapons under their
shimmering skins. Better be on my guard. When fish lurk
motionless, they look like dead people. They'll crush everything in their path.

I've loved you oh so dearly
And now my heart is sore.
I am so sad, my dearest,
Never to see you more.

(She's blind, she doesn't see the danger, they're going to attack
her, but I'll rescue her. . . .)

I knew that you would leave me,
I knew you wouldn't rest.
(I'm faithful to you, Helga. . . .)

> Grief bursts my heart asunder
> And gushes from my breast.

At breast, which Helga seemed to hold out under the noses of
the audience like a bursting one-teat udder, somebody screamed:
Holy Mary, Mother of God! And another: Shut your trap! (It's
coming, it's coming, it's starting. Bachmann clenched his fist.)

> Hear my song, Violetta,
> Hear my pleasing song!
> Come down into my gondola,
> Hear my song . . .

(In her excitement Helga had got her numbers mixed up.)

At the word gondola a blond young man with rickety teeth
jumped up and screamed: gondola, gondola, gondola! (It was
little Carlo, who recognized his native language.) Shouts
crashed like bombs. Then a voice said: Carlo, sit down. Bachmann had clenched both fists and waited.

The storm would break any minute.

Little Carlo, who was dead drunk, sat down, but popped up
a second later: Bellissima, carina . . . he sighed. His friends had
to push him down in his seat. The friend who had told Carlo
to sit down called out: Scusi, Signorina.

Carlo's whole body trembled, he buried his head in his hands
and sobbed: Mamma, Mamma . . . Beer ran down his open
shirt. When the hall was quiet again, Helga completed the last
line and sang a loud "my pleading song!"

Helga responded nervously to the ovation and stepped down
from the platform. Janko, who saw that his plans had been
thwarted, was furious with her for mixing up her songs. He
tapped his bow to stop the applause. A hush followed. Suddenly Carlo jumped up, ran through the hall, knocking over
glasses and chairs, and fell on his knees in front of Helga.

He picked up the hem of her dress, giving everyone a view of her blotchy red legs up to the knees, and burbled (Bachmann stood up, prepared to step in), I'm from Venice and we have gondolas. Venezia. Anche bella. Venezia, golden Venezia. (He kissed the floor at Helga's feet as if it had been the stones of his beloved city.) Three hundred candles for my San Stefano as true as I'm kneeling here, three hundred candles if I see my city again. Lousy Germany! His four friends stood there helplessly, darting frightened glances around them. They were aware of the danger. Bachmann had taken a step forward: If he bites her foot, I'll jump him.

Janko gave Carlo a light tap with his violin bow and said in Italian: Beat it, go home, you drunken pig. He raised his bow, turned to his Gypsies and ordered: Csardas!

Enrico, Carlo's cousin, gave Janko a tap on the shoulder. When Janko turned around, he wrenched the bow out of his hand and broke it over his knee.

Here, you son of a bitch, let's see what you can do with it now. Nobody's going to touch my brother. Lousy Germany! He's right!

Enrico, cosa fai? cried the tall pale Armando. Enrico pushed Armando away and held the weeping Carlo to his breast. He shouted: They herded us here like dogs, no, like rats. God will punish them, He'll send His fire to burn them up, every last one of them. Don't cry, Carlo, the time will come. Aha, it flashed through Bachmann's mind, he admits it, he's calling them to battle. They want to chew the whale to pieces, one step closer to Helga and I'll strangle him. I'm keeping my eyes open.

Mirko Janko also saw the danger of the situation. If you don't show you're not part of this scum, everybody will think you're in cahoots with them. Break my bow! The dirty dog! I'll show that dago.

He took a chair and brought it down with a crash on Enrico's skull. Enrico lost his balance and fell. Armando gave the signal for a counterattack: Swine! Traitors! Ass lickers!

Only the foreigners took part in the battle. The Dutchmen sided with the Italians, the Belgians and Czechs with Janko. A flying beer glass knocked Hitler's picture off the wall behind the bar. Out in the street a woman's voice screamed: Police! Help! Police!

That was the Mother Brown Bear, Frau Grimzek. Herr Grimzek was phoning in the backroom.

Carlo lay unconscious. Helga knelt down beside him, felt his forehead and screamed through the noise: Hurry, first aid, he's dead.

When the blue disappeared from his field of vision, Bachmann went into action. He took two steps forward. I've got to hold myself in check, he said to himself over and over. My grip is as hard as steel. The battle went on. Helga screamed again: He's dead. But Janko throttled Enrico and roared: Satan! Macaroni!

Armando pounded a Belgian to the floor with both fists: Dog! Monkey shit! Motherfucker!

Help! Helga screamed, help, and refused to surface. BREAK IT UP! The voice was so loud that the people around him stopped their ears. The infantrymen saluted, for the giant who pushed through the cloud like a mammoth was wearing the silver braid of a sergeant. Everyone froze. Bachmann helped Helga to her feet. Everyone present thought they were dreaming. The sergeant was half a head taller than Helga. They'd never seen anything like it. Some pushed forward for fear of missing any part of the spectacle.

He's dead, said Helga.

Bachmann put his left ear to Carlo's chest and slowly stood up. Bosh, he announced.

Still no one moved. Little Carlo, who was lying somewhere between the hoofs of the two monsters, seemed forgotten. The crowd was waiting tensely for the show to begin. Even the Italians couldn't summon up breath for a sigh of relief. Mirko Janko held a handkerchief over his left eye and with his right looked alternately at Helga and the giant. The devil take him, he cursed (inaudibly). His swollen left eye pinched him with jealousy. Christ Almighty, Janko growled to himself, if I could only speak my mind.

Bachmann had hardly given him a glance. He bent down and pulled Carlo up by one arm, and when Carlo's legs wouldn't hold him, Helga took the other arm. It looked as if the two giants were trying to divide up the little Italian between them. Carlo teetered and his head hung down to one side. Saliva was running out of his mouth. Just look at this man, Bachmann droned, you ought to be ashamed of yourself. You almost killed him with your brawling. Your conduct is an insult to human reason. All conflicts can be settled peaceably. It's disgraceful.

The Germans gaped. Those elegant high-flown words frightened them. The foreigners understood only that the soldier was taking the poor fellow under his wing. Only the people in the back rows ventured to titter. Helga hung spellbound on her Bachmann's lips. Here, said Bachmann to Enrico, and handed him back his friend, like a professor returning an exhibit to his assistant after a lecture, here, take him home. Bachmann wiped his hands on his uniform. Mirko Janko was seething with rage, because in the presence of this ox Helga lost her self-assurance.

As a Bulgarian, Mirko knew, he had certain advantages over the German. He had risked the reputation of his band by letting this whore sing, but not so she should go to bed with this big brute. Which she'll probably do this very night. He quaked with fury. His good eye blinked nervously. His fear of the Gestapo and the Labor Office evaporated. Jealousy and passion were stronger. Lousy Germany. Rotten Fascist scum, he hissed inaudibly between his teeth. In his helpless rage against the German, he looked on the Italians as brothers. He took a step toward Enrico. Everybody expected murder, but Mirko took Enrico's face in his hands and kissed him on both cheeks: Forgive me, my friend, he said and held out his hand, it was all a misunderstanding. Enrico hesitated a moment, then he saw the sincerity in Mirko's eyes. He returned the kiss and said: Ah, we're all drunk. The company was caught up in a wave of brotherly love. A moment before they had been punching and kicking, now they fell on each other's necks. Hands were shaken, cheeks kissed, hair stroked.

Bravo! cried the Sergeant, that's what I like to see. Peace is the best thing. Everybody shouted hurrah. Drinks all around on me, Mirko roared, and began clearing the platform. Voices at the entrance whispered: police. The word shot through the entire clientele of the Bear like an electric shock. Solemnly, like high priests, two policemen entered. The crowd opened up a path. Behind the policemen came a glowering Grimzek and planted himself in front of Carlo, who was lying on a bench, moaning. He started it, Grimzek declared.

Mirko Janko tried his sunniest smile: Come, come, he was drunk. The crowd responded in chorus with a murmur of sympathy for the wounded Italian.

Quiet! cried the policeman. Who insulted the Reich? Silence. I repeat: Who. . . ? He turned to Mirko. Nobody, said Mirko Janko, nobody around here is that crazy.

Maria pushed up from the second row. It was him, she yelled, pointing to Carlo who was just waking up. He's innocent, Enrico shouted, moving in front of his friend. Maria poked a finger into Enrico's stomach. You too, she said. If you don't like it here, why don't you go home? Who needs you around here?

The sergeant turned to Maria: you weren't even here, hold your tongue. That was too much for Skinny Maria. She'd been there since two in the afternoon. She was there every day. The Brown Bear was her second home. She wasn't going to take any guff from this ox. That's a lie, she screamed savagely. What are you doing here anyway? You ought to be at the front. Lounging around at home when men are dying out there. She had recovered from the melancholy inspired by Helga's song. Bachmann grinned: She's right, perfectly right. My place is at the front. Everybody laughed at the good joke and applauded the quick repartee. It's no joke. The woman is right. That's what I've been telling the board for months. I ought to be at the front. And not at home. Some laughed again at the sly humor, others began to look solemn. Maria, who saw that there was no point arguing with this lout, turned around to Mirko Janko. She had accounts to settle with him, and this was the time. Every time she had a suggestion for the request program, he played deaf. But now I'll tell him off: You scum, she bellowed into his face (Mirko took a step backward, almost bowled over by the rotgut fumes from her toothless mouth), you only came to Germany to rape our girls. First you play something to make them weak, and then you go hoopla. She gestured with both hands to make the nature of a Bulgarian hoopla perfectly clear. A few of the bystanders tried to pacify Maria, it was hopeless. Her hatred poured out like dishwater. The whole Reich was swarming with foreigners. Wherever you go, all you hear is foreign gobbledygook. Chop, chop, choop, choop. Always plotting together. Who invited you anyway? That was one question Janko had no desire to answer, for Janko had come to Germany voluntarily with his band, at home he'd have been sent to the Army. He was beginning to feel very uncomfortable. He regretted his reconciliation with the Italians and cursed his passion for Helga. Bachmann, who had no inkling of Mirko's hatred for him, put in: A foreigner is a long way from home, you shouldn't be mean to him. It's not nice. Every one of these fine men is helping us to fight the war.

He glanced over at Mirko, expecting a look of gratitude, but Mirko averted his eyes.

They're spies, Maria screamed.

Who insulted the Reich? Out with it! The policeman yelled. But since no one except Skinny Maria stepped forward (and she stank so powerfully of alcohol that it took his breath away), he turned to the sergeant and Helga: You and you, come along to the police station to testify. I want to testify, Maria cried indignantly. My husband and my two sons died for their country. There were tears in her eyes. I'll testify all right, don't worry. My three men are dead and I haven't any left. So foreigners can eat their bellies full in the Reich, she sobbed, that's what they had to die for.

That's enough now, Maria, said Herr Grimzek. He could tell by the policeman's face that Maria wasn't making a favorable impression, shut up now or I'll throw you out. You were never married to Fritz, and you had your sons with a lot of tramps.

Maria was beside herself. She bellowed like a wounded animal: But I brought them into the world, they came out of here (she pointed to her emaciated belly). A few of the bystanders laughed. Quiet, the policeman ordered.

But Maria, against whom the whole world had conspired, refused to be intimidated. They'd taken everything from her, now she was going to get even: Nobody's going to throw me out, she fumed at Grimzek who retreated a few steps, you can't throw the wife of a German soldier out. Not you or anybody else. It was the foreign riffraff and your kind that got Germany into the war. You'll get yours. Shit on the SA. You brown murderers. My husband and my sons were in the SS, she added a little more calmly.

No politics around here! said the policeman, you over there (he pointed to the Italians and the Bulgarians), come along, and you and you (he pointed to Helga and the sergeant). O.K. Get going.

Like monks going to Mass in the middle of the night to celebrate a secret Easter festival with their Saviour, the procession of sick souls moved off toward the Temple of Justice. With the slow, hard footfalls of repentant sinners. Ahead flitted the giant shadows of Bachmann and Helga, each lost in his own mazes. Bachmann was convinced that the police knew all about Narvik, he saw drawers full of documents with nothing on them but his name. "Bachmann." Just Bachmann. He had his defense ready. This is the time to tell the truth. The pure unvarnished truth. Maybe it was chance, maybe Providence, but now the abscess has burst, let the pus drain. My military career is finished for good. When Halftan lay like a dead swallow in the snow with his wings outspread and his beak buried in the ground, I suspected as much. When Helga was a whale, the primordial mother of all living creatures, standing on the platform, breathing life into them all, the miracle happened. I saw it. The evil bird of prey (how deceptive that gray coat was!) turned into a blue mammal. The metamorphosis didn't even take a week. God loves me. He's given me a third and last chance. The heart must be repentant, the mind receptive. The hour is at hand, but He is wise and compassionate in His justice. Helga too had a number of things to ponder. The promise she had given Mirko, her career as a singer was washed up if she couldn't keep it (and now that Bachmann had turned up, it was impossible), and to make her misfortunes complete, she was five days late with her period.

The shivering figures of the Italians and Bulgarians, beaten, tired dogs (Enrico and Armando were holding Carlo up), followed the two giants, the policemen at the tail end of the procession were smoking. At a distance of thirty feet, so as not to attract attention, Skinny Maria crept after them, for she too had been seized with a passionate desire to speak the pure and ultimate truth before the highest judge.

IN THE DESERTED BAR Grimzek, his wife and the two Ukrainian helpers were cleaning up.

Grimzek let his wife and the two helpers do the work. He had something more important to attend to. With brown gummed tape, ordinarily used to reinforce the windows against bomb blast, he mended the torn picture of the Führer. He cursed all foreigners but also the government agencies that had brought them to Germany. Deep down in his heart he yearned for peace and respectable customers. But the golden party badge on his lapel interfered with his reflections, muddled his feelings. Even if he was a scoundrel and maybe even a spy, Mirko Janko had brought him customers. If not for Janko and his Gypsies the crowd would be going to the Green Huntsman or even the Father Rhine.

He'd miss Mirko. Such a loss could never be made good. The insurance company would pay for the rest of the damage, though it would be in no hurry about it. On the other hand the Reich had been insulted. Lovingly he pasted his strips on the underside of the Führer's mustache as if this would make up for his equivocal attitude. He turned his Führer over and looked into his fixed, fanatical eyes. On the one hand the man wants to save Germany from the Bolshevists, but on the other hand Grimzek sometimes had his doubts about the success of the Germanic mission. He closed his eyes, fearing that the Führer might read his secret thoughts in them. He put the picture down and looked around. Don't stand there doing nothing, he roared at his Ukrainians with recovered self-confidence. You lazy bastards, I'll teach you to lie down on the job.

The EAST painted on their backs in big letters suddenly reminded him that it was only four days until Easter and that a long-awaited shipment of Moselle wine would be delivered any day now. The wine costs 540 marks. The Führer needs a new glass: twelve marks fifty. Damn foreigners, you lose more than you take in. Herr Grimzek, whose thick snub nose actually had a certain Brown Bear quality, poured himself a double cognac and belched.

POLICE CHIEF HEINZ-OTTO MUSCHEL sat square and robust on God's Throne, to which Bachmann was bringing his repentance. Lucky for Bachmann and the rest of them that it should be Muschel, for as everyone knew, Muschel wasn't one of the worst kind. He was a mixture of bluffness and sentimentality. He was intelligent, full of ideas, and essentially shy. But he always repressed one or another aspect of his many-sided personality, and sometimes he just stared dreamily into space. At such times he was perfectly harmless. Muschel had one passion: sex. In that field his resourcefulness was amazing. A man of genius, who as so often happens had missed his calling. In a different day, in different latitudes, he would have been right-hand man to a mighty potentate. The police career offered his artistic temperament only limited possibilities, he rarely had occasion to bring his full powers into play. During office hours he held himself in check and seldom or never let himself be tempted to reveal the secret of his art. He had iron fists and knew how to use them, but he also had original ideas. To those who expected an unimaginative bureaucrat Muschel came as a distinct surprise. His colleagues, for instance, swore by the Gestapo code as set forth in the booklet: *Regulations and Penal Laws Covering Foreign Workers in the Territory of the German Reich, exclusive of Special Provisions Applicable to Hungarians, Latvians, and Frenchmen from Unoccupied France, but Including Measures Applying Specifically to Poles, Ukrainians, White Russians and Tatars, Seventh Printing*. In Muschel's opinion the booklet was gross, impractical, and unimaginative. What the Gestapo and the SS tried to accomplish with gallows or hard labor in the quarries, Muschel did much more cheaply and effectively with water. He sobered up his foreigners. From dissolute daydreams he awakened them to sobriety, which to his mind was the virtue of virtues. Killing and torturing struck him as stupid and useless. Water and threats were more rational weapons in the struggle against demoralization. Murder was inefficient barbarism.

Publicly, of course, he talked the same language as the Gestapo men who like hyenas were permanently on the lookout for victims. But in practice he did everything he could to save lives. Muschel was a civilized Western European. The thought of corpses darkened his horizon, nauseated him.

After the procession had climbed the four steps leading to the police station, a door was opened at the far end of the corridor, and Helga and Bachmann were shown into a waiting room.

The foreigners continued on into the courtyard, where they were lined up. Two policemen took a garden hose from a shed. Standing in his shirtsleeves (the police station was overheated) Heinz-Otto Muschel commanded: Water! The six Bulgarians and five Italians came close to drowning. The water lashed their faces like a cloudburst. They shivered in their drenched clothes. Mirko yelled: Stop, stop! But the stream of water gushing into his mouth (this wasn't the first time) soon silenced him.

Splendid, said Commissioner Muschel, gazing contentedly at the wet, hopping figures, that will do for this evening. Hand in your identification papers, you will be called one by one for questioning. The rest will wait outside until their names are called. Have I made myself clear?

The two policemen collected the identification papers and handed them to the chief through the window.

As I live and by my mother's grave, Mirko Janko's teeth chattered, we didn't start it.

We know all about you, Janko, said Muschel. If you aren't

sent to a concentration camp for subversive activities, you'll be in luck. The least you'll get is five years in the penitentiary for crimes against morality. We don't need any public prosecutor for that. Your case is clear. The whole town knows the way you chase after German girls. I guess you thought it could go on forever. No, my friend. You don't know us. We won't stand for your perversions.

What perversions, Herr Inspector?

You expect me to run through the list to give you a thrill? Your papers will stay here until further notice. And now go home. Dismissed. Beat it! Heil Hitler! Next.

The next was Eugen Poplov, the harmonica player. I have three children in Bulgaria, please. Water and cold sweat ran down his forehead. What can I do?

Three children. So much the worse, Muschel decided. The next time your wife will show more sense in picking a husband. Anyway, let's hope so. It's a hard life for a widow with three children.

But I'm still alive, Poplov screamed in horror, for he was beginning to have his doubts. Muschel surveyed Poplov from top to toe. Yes, he said, I can see that. But none of us lives forever, Poplov. Your papers stay here. Go home now, until further notice. Mind you, I said until further notice. Dismissed. Heil Hitler! Next.

After Poplov came Koko Pirokov, the pianist. He was a plump young bachelor of twenty-three, ordinarily benign and amiable.

It was only a joke, he smiled, please. People get into a crazy mood sometimes.

A joke? Isn't that lovely! If you people have to amuse yourselves, you can tickle each other as far as I'm concerned. But the law is no laughing matter. I suppose the Reich is a joke? Koko made no reply.

Well, speak up, Muschel shouted. Is the Reich a joke?

No, said Koko and attempted a solemn expression. Of course it's no joke. I meant the fight.

You'll learn to laugh on the other side of your face, said Muschel prophetically, I'll give you that in writing. Your papers stay here for the present. That's no joke. What's that? Dismissed. Heil Hitler! Next.

Poplov, Pirokov, Zapotchki, Glukov, Grumb, Bellini, Ferrantini, Bolzago, Piramento, Spiccerini. One after another they stepped up, like shipwrecked youngsters before their rescuer, listened to his sermon and exposed themselves to Muschel's wit and Muschel's temperament. Each was threatened with the same justice, each without exception had to abandon the last semblance of an identity, his papers. Without papers you could hardly be counted among the living.

The two last Italians were given mops and buckets and instructed to mop up the floor, the stairs, and the corridor.

Though Muschel indulged in loose language and an occasional joke with foreigners (for they too were human), that didn't mean by a long shot that he was going to clean up the mess they left behind. And his esthetic sense rebelled against water, dirt, and disorder. Because of his little jokes, and because he sometimes had a fit of laughter in the middle of an interrogation, he was rather well liked and referred to almost affectionately as our Muschel, his name was uttered without the least hatred. Not only Germans, but foreign workers as well had good things to say of him. It was known, for example, that Muschel had succeeded, over the opposition of the highest authorities, in letting a Polish woman keep her newborn child. He saw to it that mother and child were sent to the same camp. Such things made an impression. Or the affair of the Rhine bargeman, who for months had delivered salt to various citizens of Honnef instead of the sugar they were expecting (a layer of sugar on top, salt underneath). They had bound him hand and foot and were about to throw him into the Rhine when Muschel unexpectedly (he always knew what was going on in his district) went into action, set the swindler free, and in the presence of his vengeful victims knocked him down, breaking his nose in the process. Unintentionally as it happened, he had wanted to knock a few teeth out. (His nose didn't amount to much in the first place, he consoled the avengers, who declared themselves satisfied with Muschel's justice.)

When the name of the witness Helga Okolek was given him (for some reason or other he had never had her in his police station before), he looked avidly among the photographs to see whether they included one of this witness. He found all sorts of people in all sorts of positions, but no one even remotely resembling the legendary Helga. Feeling glances in the back of his neck, he closed the portfolio and put it in the drawer. He opened a second, deeper drawer, removed a half-empty glass of beer, took a swallow, and put it away again. The room was overheated and it seemed to him that the two giants who were bending over him were thirsty too. He felt threatened. Come on, sit down, said Muschel. Then there was a brief silence. The beginnings of sentences were his greatest weakness. Once he started talking, it was all right, but the beginnings tried his nerves.

Muschel was really embarrassed. (Even after twenty years he hadn't entirely digested the idea that he was chief of police and entitled to unlimited respect.) Helga's breasts, bobbing big and pointed before his eyes, made his situation even more embarrassing. He cast about for a little joke to break the ice. For a gesture, however simple, that would help him through these first critical moments. At last a trusty old trick occurred to him. It had often helped. He took a pencil and wedged it between his nose and upper lip. That made him feel human again. His self-assurance swelled. Such humor on the part of an official was bound to be disarming. He was convinced that the witnesses had become an inch or two smaller. His spirits revived.

For a moment he thought of the wet Italians. Especially Carlo's terrified face when the water brought him fully to his senses, gladdened his heart, and Janko, who kept licking the water from his dripping mustache, was a scream. If he'd been alone, he'd have laughed aloud.

Keep sober, Heinz-Otto, Muschel said to himself. There's a thing or two you still have to do. With a passing glance at Helga, he turned to Bachmann: Your name?

Gauthier Bachmann.

How do you spell it?

BACHMANN, Bachmann spelled.

Not that, the first name.

GAUTHIER. It's French. Please make a note of that.

Bachmann waited until Muschel had his pencil in hand (he relaxed his upper lip and deftly caught it) before going on: Gauthier Bachmann was born on May 15, 1919 in Duisburg on the Rhine, the son of the respected master gold- and silver-smith, August Bachmann. His, that is my, father died on September 24, 1927 of a heart attack. Exactly on his sixty-fifth birthday. To the day of his death in full possession of his mental faculties. His, that is my, people came originally from Flanders.

I beg your pardon, Muschel interrupted, in the first place, you're going too far back, and in the second place I don't understand why you keep talking of yourself in the third person. It's confusing. When you say he, I hope you mean yourself. Or do you mean your father when you say me?

When I say he, said Bachmann, annoyed that the man had so rudely interrupted him, I mean him of course. We're an old, old family. My ancestors came from Flanders. The first Bach-

mann was called Beekman. Cornelius Bertram to be exact. He
was a guild master in Ghent. That accounts for the Flemish
names. In 1586 he fled to Cologne from the Reformation. Died
in 1594. His sons Frederik and Janus, respected citizens of
Cologne, were already called Bachmann like myself. Gold- and
silversmiths every one of them. The whole line down to myself.
He too is a gold- and silversmith. Last male descendant. That's
me. Had to swear an oath at my father's deathbed. That oath is
secret.

You swore a secret oath? Are your superior officers aware of
that?

I'll come back to that, said Bachmann unswervingly, the oath
in any case is an oath of loyalty to our craft, to our guild and
to Flanders, home of the Beekmans. He passed his journeyman's
examination, with honorable mention I might add, on October
14, 1937. A silver candelabrum. Master examination when the
war is over. He knows what he owes his name, and so do I.

You're mixing everything up, Herr Bachmann. I've never
heard such a hodgepodge. I hope you've got it straight yourself.
I is he, he is I, me is him, and you is also he.

It's you that's mixing things up, not I. Everything I've been
saying is perfectly clear to me even if he does confuse him and
me . . .

In any case, Herr Bachmann, said Muschel, who had never
had such an experience, you're not a bad talker. Most of it has
nothing to do with the case, but that doesn't matter. It's breath-
taking. How did you ever get to be a sergeant?

I can tell you that, too, but I must ask you not to interrupt
me. On October 22, 1941 my battery was in the Voroshenko
sector, in a fir woods. It was six in the morning. The fir woods
were two acres deep and five acres wide. Oh, yes. Just a second.
The commanding officer . . . yes, it was Lieutenant Eberhard
Fähnrich. That's right. Just a second. I've got it. I had been

recommended to Sergeant Erlang as a first-class soldier. That's a fact. (In speaking Bachmann passed his hand over his forehead as though rubbing events out of his skin.) A first-class soldier because of my size, my dexterity in close combat, and the third thing I don't remember. I think it was the gold sharpshooter badge. Anyway we were waiting to counterattack. Six o'clock. Six fifteen. Six twenty. Nothing happened. Absolutely nothing. It was a snappy autumn morning and we were all taking deep breaths, and then all of a sudden the command came: Advance. (Bachmann was speaking more and more slowly.) Then, then came a hail of shells and then we were stuck in this mud that nobody had noticed before. Most of the men were so deep in the mud, all you could see was their hands or feet or their tongues, yes tongues, and then suddenly it was all over.

What do you mean all over, Herr Bachmann?

All over. Just what I said. All over.

And that's how you got to be a sergeant?

No, of course not. I was a sergeant already. But in Voroshenko it was all over. Seven hundred and sixty-three in the first five minutes. All in the mud. Killed.

Good, that'll do, Herr Bachmann, I understand.

Muschel suspected that this man had something wrong with him, but he didn't want to make things too easy for him. The whole story left him cold, but he didn't care for this disorganized way of telling it.

Bachmann, who liked to talk about the mud of Voroshenko (and indeed it was his favorite topic), was delighted with the next question: How deep would you say that mud was, approximately?

Approximately ten to twelve feet.

Ten to twelve feet? Aren't you exaggerating a little?

Not at all. Where could seven hundred and sixty-three sol-

diers have disappeared to otherwise? And all in five minutes.
There's no doubt about it. At least ten to twelve feet deep. If
not deeper. Don't you agree?

Maybe so, said Muschel, the weather is wretched in Voroshenko at that season. It's dry and wet.

You've hit the nail on the head, said Bachmann eagerly. One
day dry, the next wet.

Exactly. You've taken the words out of my mouth. Muschel
examined Bachmann at length. Bachmann's little blue eyes were
darting uncertainly back and forth. There was something on the
tip of his tongue, but it wouldn't come out. He'd said something
that he'd have liked to clarify. But he couldn't remember what
it was. He would gladly have talked for hours, but just then he
could think of nothing to say. Muschel for his part didn't know
what to do with this pedantic gorilla. He bored him.

He looked across at Helga, studying the possibilities that
Helga's breasts would have offered that Gypsy Janko (in
Muschel's eyes all Yugoslavs, Greeks, Hungarians, and Bulgarians were Gypsies). Seen from close up, Helga's breasts were
even bigger than the reputation that preceded them. And Janko
had almost got his hands on them. But I've put a crimp in his
game. Without papers he's a corpse waiting to be buried. Now
I'll have to get this giant out of the way.

Well, well. Just keep calm. Everything in due time. Sober
does it, Heinz-Otto. Here's what we'll do: Let this fellow spend
the night with her, why not, a couple like that, it's titillating to
think of them together, but tomorrow morning the Gram
woman will be notified. She hasn't given her notice yet, but
tomorrow she will and that makes two birds with one stone.
Gram drops a hint that I was behind it, and our little bunny
rabbit comes running to me and sits up on her hind legs begging
me to straighten things out. In a case like that one good turn
deserves another. Man, won't that be something! He rubbed

his hands under his desk and smiled. A juicy deal. What's the old saying? You've got a deal when two people have something to offer each other. And while Bachmann was still immersed in the mud of Voroshenko, here and there shouting "deep," "thick," "black," "stinks," Muschel was immersed in Helga's breasts and would gladly have gone to sleep right there. Something inside him was babbling blissfully and biting giant nipples with toothless jaws. He made smacking sounds in accompaniment. What brought you to the Bear? What did you hear in the Bear?

Hear? I couldn't hear a thing. Mirko Janko was playing like mad, judged as light music it isn't bad at all. I entered the premises at eight fifteen with the intention of meeting Fräulein Helga Okolek, after spending the last four months on combat duty. (He looked around to see if anyone had caught him in his lie.) In any event I was away for four months. Then he came back. The Prodigal Son. The homeland called. The girl was waiting. I mean I came back. I've been through a lot. A world of experience.

When I opened the door: music. Stars of home, the sky glittering like diamonds. I've seen a lot of stars. In the North they're different from the South. I've been all over. From Palermo to Narvik. Sky wherever you go. But the stars of home glitter like diamonds. The Gypsy band was terrific. I was dazed. Grimzek was belching.

Yes, that's the man's name, said Muschel to conceal his sojourn on Helga's thighs.

Muschel felt a void in the pit of his stomach as though he had been pumped empty. Bachmann's pedantry and his persistent confusion of the first and third person were driving him mad.

But Bachmann was in his element. For him talking was a tranquilizer: Well then, he arrived at eight-fifteen and was sitting there over his beer. Mulling things over. It's quite a

change from the icy wastes of the North Pole to the cozy
warmth of a German inn. Inside and outside. A big difference.
You want to get up and go. But there's no going back. Never
again. Never again, I tell you.

That's enough, Herr Bachmann, enough! Muschel screamed
and held his ears. Who yelled "Lousy Germany," you can save
the rest.

I was defoaming my beer when someone shouted "Lousy
Germany."

You were doing what?

Defoaming my beer. Beer has to be defoamed. The word is
German. You look at me as if I were crazy. Of course it's German, just like foam. Perhaps not quite so current in this region,
actually quite a few things are different around here.

Muschel felt physical disgust toward this giant.

He had never imagined how painful somebody else's madness
could be. Two aspirins, he cried out, and make it quick. For
God's sake, was it the Italian or the Bulgarian who said "Lousy
Germany," you're driving me crazy. I don't know, said Bachmann
very softly, the beer got into my nose. I was just removing the
beer from my nose.

What beer? What nose?

I got it in my nose, I must have bent forward too far. Everything must be done with moderation. I did it too quickly, that
was a mistake. We make mistakes. A good many mistakes, and
later on we regret them.

Silence! Muschel commanded. I don't want to hear any more
about it. It doesn't interest me. Say what you please, but stick
to the point. I'm not sitting here for my pleasure. He opened
his collar and wiped the sweat from his forehead. He could
have thrown Bachmann out, but he was still looking forward
to a little fun with Helga.

He wanted to throw him out and to keep him. To throw

him out because Bachmann's chatter pained him, to keep him because the later it got the more surely Bachmann would spend the night at Helga's. He'd have liked best to make him stand at the window (with his back to the room of course).

I was looking toward the platform, my nose was clear again, when I heard for the second time: Lousy Germany. Oh oh, I say to myself, somebody's up to something. Fräulein Helga is in danger. I was ready to step in. But I was too late. We're often too late in life, same as in love or death for that matter.

I refuse to listen to such nonsense, Herr Bachmann, who picked up the chair? An Italian or a Bulgarian? And who yelled "Lousy Germany" the second time, that's what I want to know. Bachmann whispered almost inaudibly: The second time someone cut off my view.

Well, thank the Lord, Muschel rubbed his forehead with relief. Thank the Lord, just as I imagined. You didn't see a thing and you don't know beans. Good. So that's settled. We'll draw up the statement ourselves. Thank you. And now do what you please. Say anything that comes into your head. I'll register every word. (Muschel was glad to be able to go back to Helga.)

Good. Then I'll begin where I please. With my confession. I have to make a confession. You probably know all about it already. I have committed terrible crimes. First beheading Schnotz because he was sticking out of the hole, which wasn't my fault, the soup mixer and the seminary put me up to it. Mürz behaved like a swine too, swiped my shoes before the execution and selling them back to me for ten marks, a dirty trick, wouldn't you say? And now I still owe him the ten marks—you can't go on the firing squad barefoot, he says—that's Master Sergeant Mürz, the scoundrel. Von Göritz wasn't much better. He was a big disappointment to me. The bastard sent me to Narvik and after the contemptible behavior of Hupfen or whatever his name is, anyway it begins with Hupfen, the out-

come was inevitable. I honestly thought the world had conspired against me. I was absolutely convinced that everybody
was out to humiliate me and push me aside, but now (Bachmann raised his voice) I know it. They wanted to humiliate me
and push me aside, they knew what I didn't know, but know
now. And they were banking on it. That I'm sick. And they all
used the sick man for their own ends. They abused me!

Stop, Muschel shouted, stop! I'm not interested in your sex
life.

Everybody abused me, everybody. In his agitation Bachmann
pounded the desk with his fist. That Halftan, the dirty dog, he
seduced me like a child. Afterward he said he'd wanted to
prove that a soldier would do anything. A soldier is nothing
but a catamite in the asshole of the nation. What's that? It's
disgusting. The officers are the cocks, now I know what's what,
and the soldiers have to oblige. That's perversion! (Bachmann
pounded the table again.) Murdering four people for no reason
at all—how can a normal human being do such a thing? I
can't understand it. It's a mystery. A nation of queers. Women
are neglected, children are washed away like seeds—and
destroyed. It's disgraceful. Well, luckily my conscience woke up
after that night. I came to my senses. I REALIZE THAT I'M SICK.
I've got to undergo treatment. I've got to. The way I am they
can't punish me, nobody'll take me seriously.

He's a good man, Helga said to herself, he lies like a newspaper, but he means well. A nation of queers—that's an
exaggeration. I ought to know. He means Lesbians. There are
plenty of them. But isn't he dishing it out! My baby.

She loved Bachmann. Nothing had come of it last time,
because he'd fallen asleep on the bed, but wasn't that proof
enough that their relationship was something out of the
ordinary? A good three inches taller than me, good family and
unmarried. Fate brought us together (Helga believed in fate as

she believed in God). We belong together, like the wind and the sea. . . . Her bowels were tight with happiness (or was it Mirko's slivovitz). She felt sick to her stomach from the sausage she had eaten for supper. Her nausea was tinged with melancholy, because this Bachmann is unpredictable, and what can I do if he takes it into his head to clear out tomorrow? Her lovely large dark-brown eyes grew sad. She was sitting on the shore of a lake (the Starnberger See, that she had dreamed of so often, where she wanted to live with Bachmann and five little Bachmanns) and singing with a voice that caught in the fish nets:

The wind and the waves, ah me (sang the voice in Helga)
my sweetheart has gone, gone,
the autumn leaves are drying,
the boat is drifting away,
the wind and the waves, o sorrow,
my darling is breaking my heart,
he lies deep down in the lake.

Bachmann wasn't in the lake by any means, it was Muschel who was rummaging around in Helga's seaweed and creepers, letting out an occasional grunt. Bachmann was out to dispel the last vestiges of his guilt. Germany's full of chestnuts, he shouted, and we live on rotten meat. The consequence: We're all full to the brim with corpses, only animals so far, but it won't be long before we start in on human corpses. Right now we've got hoofs sticking out of our asses! (Helga laughed aloud: what horrid ideas he has) because we stuff ourselves like pigs!

It's a pleasure, I admit, but it can't go on. My eyes have been opened. I've seen a lot of things. I can only tell you that either something has got to happen soon or nothing will happen. If nothing happens, tongues will grow out of our ears. Halftan thought that jewels were gods on earth, and what happens: shoots himself in an open field with his ravished bride. That's what comes of it.

Schnotz thought he could poison a cook with piptol. What happens? He gets shot from behind in a quarry. They all die in Purgatory, but Gauthier Bachmann passes right through like a burned match, he survives every battle, and nobody harms a hair of his head. I can only conclude that something must be wrong with me. That's why he's got to be on his guard. Schnotz was right, as a horse I could amount to something—as a man, I may as well face it, he's, that is I am, a manure pile that breathes. I've never learned the high art of self-deception. I have no illusions. We're walking on a tightrope, but it's not a rope so help me, it's a thread. There aren't any nets. Anybody who falls is going to crack his head. I'm a sick animal by the name of Gauthier Bachmann, absolutely unfit. Women are swamps you sink into, men are stones you break against.

I'm neither above nor below, are you some place where I'm not?

Bachmann suddenly fell on his knees, clasped his hands and said softly: Forgive me please, forgive me. He stood up just as quickly and sat down as if nothing had happened.

Me? asked Muschel with a start, where I am? I'm right here. (That's a lie, in reality Muschel was between Helga's large full lips and he didn't want any half-wit to interrupt him.) I'm the Honnef police chief. I've noted everything you said, word for word. Up here (he pointed to his forehead), it's all registered up here. Incidentally, I must ask you to discontinue those knee bends.

It's all one to me, Bachmann continued, growing redder and redder in the face, anyway I'm going back to the hospital I escaped from and let them cure me. In Voroshenko something hit me in the head, see the scar?—because I was an ass, I stuck my bean out of the swamp. If I hadn't done that, I'd have drowned and it wouldn't have happened. But it's no use crying over spilt milk. I've got to get well quickly. Because soon the war will be over, then I'll be a pacifist and I never want to hear another word about war and soldiers. Cured or uncured, I've had enough. My kind of men are pacifists. But cured is better. What about you? Have you made your choice?

Muschel had just come to the panties and had a hard time choosing. Blue, pink, black or white. White is still very common with girls of her type. Most likely they're white. White naturally led him to the opposite. Black. Black was Muschel's color. He'd figured it out very cleverly. He was so fond of black that he couldn't strip them off. All right, let them be white again. That's perfect, Heinz-Otto. Just what you wanted. And to cut the knot he added thick wool to the white, because white and thick wool didn't appeal to him in the least. This done, there was no obstacle to stripping off her panties. The vision that presented itself before he was half through parched his lips, but when he beheld her giant buttocks, white, soft and well rounded, he had to close his eyes for a short moment. His breath failed him. Herr Bachmann, he wheezed, there's no hurry about getting cured (haste makes waste, he wrote).

Anyway, Bachmann concluded his testimony, when I heard the young lady screaming "Help, he's dead," I stood up and yelled: "Break it up."

What's that? Break it up? Muschel asked with clouded eyes.

Not like that, said Bachmann, like this. He stood up and roared: Break it up! Every windowpane in the place trembled. The two policemen in the next room stuck their heads in, they looked very pale.

What's the matter? Bachmann asked. Did I frighten you? I have a healthy voice, the rest of me is contaminated.

Helga's voice fluttered (so she thought) like a canary in a cage. The part of her body that Muschel had saved for the last was in flames. She was so proud of Bachmann she'd have liked to hug and kiss him. He's much better than stupid old Jannings. I'll stay with you, my sweetheart. I'll do everything for you. Five little Bachmanns playing ring around a rosy. In our house on the Starnberger See. Juchhe! O my sweet darling. My angel. Again she was overcome with joy, but again it gave her heartburn.

Herr Bachmann, did you know Fräulein Okolek before?

Oh yes, certainly I knew her (with a smile and a motion of the hand), but only superficially. See what I mean. But that's going to be changed very soon.

I hope you made out all right, said Muschel, and wrote "make out" on another slip of paper.

I'll make out all right, said Bachmann and looked at Muschel challengingly.

Muschel's mouth was watering, it's been a pleasant evening and it's getting better and better. And tomorrow night will . . .

He turned to Helga with a severe look (he thought severity would bring better results) but Bachmann, who hadn't felt so good in a long time, wanted to put in a good word for the poor foreigners: Herr Polizeikommissar. Those foreigners you had in here are only poor devils, let them go.

Muschel scrutinized Bachmann, trying to discover some sign of complicity on the part of a German citizen with foreigners suspected of hostility to the Reich. Detecting nothing of the kind (according to the REGULATIONS a German of this sort betrayed himself by conspicuous movements of the Adam's apple, according to Muschel by a slight blush and Bachmann's face was a milky white) Muschel said: Herr Bachmann, do I look like a monster? Does a monster look like me? No, and I'm not a bureaucrat either. I'm a human being myself and, as the poet said, nothing human is alien to me. What interests me is the human element. I am first and foremost a pedagogue. In a labor training camp they teach these foreign rascals some sense. No other Reich agency can do that as well as a camp, because a camp has the right kind of teachers for the job, which isn't an easy one by God. Of course, nothing a handful of drunken foreigners say can insult the Reich, that's nonsense, but any foreigner who is unable to behave like a normal German, who rebels and raises hell, has to be brought to his senses. You must realize that, Herr Bachmann.

Bachmann understood at once what Muschel was driving at, he wanted to send the foreigners to some kind of military installation. Though military installations had lost their attraction for him personally (he was all for hospitals now), he felt they were too good for foreigners. His memory of the good old days (of the theological seminary for instance, before that stupid incident with Schnotz) hadn't entirely paled. My advice is two weeks of confinement to quarters, then send them to a hospital and tie them to their beds for three weeks. Spread a man's arms out for a few weeks like, forgive the comparison, our Saviour on the Cross, and he'll lose all desire to raise hell. Take it from me.

Conceivably, said Muschel. That may be true in certain cases, but I personally wouldn't expect too much from that crucified position. It might temporarily discourage them from masturbating, which between you and me is a common habit with foreigners. But the second you untie them, they'll start raising hell again.

Stop, Bachmann interrupted. Have you a grudge against foreigners? It certainly sounds that way.

A grudge against foreigners? Me? Muschel's face was all astonishment. How could anyone conceive such a preposterous idea! No, certainly not. You may not believe me, but I like them. I even envy them. We Germans, we may as well admit it, are provincial by comparison. Don't you agree? No, Herr Bachmann, on the contrary. Take the Italians—a nation of artists, or the French—that's the mind at its best, it's only in France that you find really intelligent people, or the English—what a wealth of tradition, what cool courage—or the Dutch? A clean, modern country. What are we by comparison? Thinkers and poets, soldiers and technicians, all very well, but . . . how German, how typically German! See what I mean? But for goodness' sake don't get me wrong, now you'll begin to think I'm against us . . . how could I be? I'm a German myself.

You've convinced me, said Bachmann, he could see by Muschel's face that he was telling the truth. You personally are not opposed to foreigners.

Of course not, it's clear as day . . . but the fact is that the Gestapo can handle those fellows better than we can. . . . They have experience. (The best method of course is a cold bath, Muschel reflected, but he didn't wish to air his distaste for the Gestapo, put them in ice-cold water up to their chins for three days and they'll eat out of your hand.)

Well then, Herr Bachmann, I see that it's two o'clock. You've spoken well, when you're dead and buried, roses will sprout from your mouth, as the poet would say. We may send for you again.

When I'm dead, Bachmann smiled, I'll turn to stone. We're all stones, we can't die, we're all dead already. I've got used to it. I'm not alone as I used to be. Now that I know how sick I am, I'm not lonely any more. I belong. This is something more than a national brotherhood. It's humanity. It doesn't matter any more where a man comes from. We're a huge pile of stones. A pyramid or a quarry. White cliffs. We were never born. Stones of every conceivable color and degree of hardness: *that's universal humanity.* Poor and rich, young and old, healthy and sick—we all belong together. The metamorphosis took place long ago, only most people haven't caught on. The people who haven't found out call themselves normal. But men aren't stones. That is, we're not what we are. In other words, they're all sick like me. Gold has turned to dirt, man to animal, animal to stone, and from stone gunpowder and dust are made. Roses are sprouting from my mouth and every other orifice right now, you don't have to wait until later.

Strange, strange indeed, Muschel shook his head. I get weird ideas too: Every day when the dawn comes, it happens at night in the summertime, I wake up and see the light and I think my last day is beginning. I can hardly open my eyes, but I can't get back to sleep. A hundred pounds of dead weight pulling at every muscle. What can it be?

I don't know, said Bachmann, but when I'm cured, I'll be as light as a feather, I'll float like a cloud. But God save us from holes in the ground, from traps and snares.

He's trying to spoil my evening, Muschel thought. But he won't succeed. I listen to him, but he ignores me. Oh well, he's the witness, not me.

Fräulein Helga, he asked sternly and with a look of exasperation, I'm ready to hear your testimony.

Helga parted her lips. (Built for sucking. Tomorrow night, Heinz-Otto, along about seven o'clock, you're going to take half a dozen eggs and toss them into the frying pan.) All right, go ahead, and don't beat around the bush.

Helga shrugged her shoulders: They were all drunk. I wouldn't take it seriously.

That's not for you to say, Fräulein Helga Okolek, kindly let the police decide what's to be taken seriously. Just stick to the facts.

My goodness, if we paid attention to everything those foreigners say among themselves. We can't understand them anyway. To tell you the honest truth, I have a feeling that they're not in love with us.

Muschel's severity wasn't to Helga's liking. What are you trying to hide, Fräulein, will you kindly come to the point?

This bald-headed fellow was making her sick. What does he want of me?

Those people only work for us, am I right, they don't belong to us. When a hen cackles, nobody asks if she likes to lay eggs. We had cows at home, it didn't hurt us any when they mooed at each other in the barn.

To the point, Fräulein Helga.

All right. To the point. Mirko Janko asked me if I'd sing for his band. I love to sing. Aside from that, what happens in the Bear is none of my business. Indifference was no use to Muschel. He needed excitement. I'll warm her up a bit. That's no proper attitude for a German girl, he bellowed at her. The Reich is every German's business. Everybody knows that. Helga shrugged her shoulders again and stood up. I'm not going to sit here and let that idiot yell at me. When Helga was standing behind her chair, Muschel had the closeup shot he needed. In color. What a magnificent hunk of woman. And only sixteen. Juicy and round as a big peach. Imagine biting off a piece. Put boots on her and give her a whip—I think I've got the right size for her—with those muscles. He felt the welts on his back and behind. A part of him was beginning to stir. (It's high time—that hermaphrodite in uniform almost put me to sleep.) I think we'll keep you here for the night, said Muschel slowly. Every syllable was calculated. But the violence of the reaction took him by surprise.

Me? Helga screamed. Me? Oh no, you won't. I have nothing to testify about. I don't rat on anybody. Her eyes blazed with fury. Go get Skinny Maria, she's only waiting to shoot off her mouth, you won't get a damn thing out of me.

Come come. This outburst was almost too much.

He wanted to stand up too but was afraid his excitement would be too conspicuous. Not here in the police station. That wouldn't do. In his own home he wouldn't have minded, on the contrary. But in his official capacity he had to maintain a certain dignity. He prepared to strike the final blow, for it was only a matter of seconds. And then, said Muschel lasciviously, you'll be sent home to your parents.

Fear of her pious mother, who was always counting her rosary and leaving her false teeth lying around, the thought of her home that smelled of onions and warmed-up leftovers, made Helga furious. She leaped forward like a mortally wounded elephant.

You, you can . . . (she hesitated, she didn't dare).

Yes, Muschel implored, with a last effort at self-control, what can I?

. . . kiss my ass! Helga screamed and bit her lips.

Muschel's release knew no bounds. A flood, a deluge. For a moment he closed his eyes. Helga, and Bachmann as well, feared the worst, they expected him to arrest them on the spot. Instead, a thin, weary voice sighed: Thank you, Fräulein Oko-lek, thank you. And in utter exhaustion he whispered: You may go now. Heil Hitler!

Helga and Bachmann weren't the only ones. The two police-men, who were looking through the door again, were equally flabbergasted. What an extraordinary conclusion for one of Mus-chel's interrogations! Get moving! Muschel commanded, get out and make it fast. He'd have liked to throw the policemen out too. Get out! Bachmann and Helga left the police station. Outside they caught their breath. The heat in the police station had been stifling.

I can tell you who the scoundrels were. I was there all evening, I was at the Bear from two o'clock on. (This was Maria, who, as soon as she heard the others leaving, popped out of the waiting room as a rat darts from its hole, and rushed into the guardroom.) I can testify (her voice cracked). They all cursed the Reich. They've been doing it for years. Every one of them. The whole gang. They're all in the same boat. Shoot them! Shoot them!

Get out! came Muschel's voice. Get out, I tell you! You drunken whore. I've had enough for tonight. I don't need you.

And before the Throne of God the door slammed.

As they walked in silence to Alfred-Rosenberg-Platz, back down the endless Hauptstrasse, they resembled a dinosaur couple emerging from the water to hunt for living prey in a landscape peopled exclusively by stone plants.

MUSCHEL HAD DONE IT. When they reached the house door, Bachmann had no choice, and for Helga everything was finished anyway. Four gigantic shoes stood like unmasted toy ships behind the door, but Helga who sat beside Bachmann on the bed had no other feeling than fear. A year before Frau Gram had picked her up in a waiting room—Helga was on her way to Hamburg, but didn't have the fare—and offered her an attic room free of charge. The year had passed like a summer season, the shops were closing, the deck chairs had been put away, the beach umbrellas were gone. And here I am out on the street. It's all over with the singing. She doesn't want me to pay the price. As far as my womanhood is concerned, I've got nothing to lose. But it's all the same to her. Normal men have never loved me, but I take pity on all men. Maybe because she doesn't want to take pity on me. Who knows? And this Bachmann? You call that a man? First he goes chasing around the world looking for a regiment, and when he comes home, all he can think of is going to the hospital. When you're six feet tall, you don't get a normal man. It can't be helped. She looked down at Bachmann who lay on the bed like a stone, staring at the light bulb. He seemed to her now like a sickening caricature of herself. Her grotesqueness had duplicated itself. We ought to be in a circus. She shuddered. And I had been waiting for this. I longed for him. Bachmann had taken his coat off and covered himself up with it, his big flat face emerged from the field gray like the face of a corpse in an open coffin. Only the whites of his eyes showed, the pupils had vanished, now they were black dots on the yellow lamp shade. Helga longed for a bad air raid. They go all over, but they never come here. Every day a few

164

cities burn down, but Honnef, God knows why, is spared. Ten thousand bombers and a hundred thousand tons of explosives and the whole shit will be over. I won't have to bring any bastards into the world, I won't need any room or any Bachmann. Or Janko or a career.

Ten thousand bombers. And no more fear of Gram and Muschel. Spiders looking for prey. The one violent, the other fragrant.

Spinning their nets and sucking my blood. Helga had lost interest in everything, especially Bachmann. She was cold. Though she wanted to die, she was afraid of the silence. Lies there like a corpse and doesn't give a damn what happens to me.

What are you looking at?

She had to repeat her question. What is there to look at up there?

I always see the same thing. I thought it was gone. But it keeps coming back. Bachmann's voice came out of a well. Always the same thing. Chains of mountains, woods, lakes, fields. It's boring. Always the same. It's painful. Rolling hills, an endless landscape. It makes me sick.

Mountains too, Gauthier?

Mountains most of all.

And little birch woods?

Woods are unbearable. Even the smallest forests are too big. The smallest trees are too tall. And all those weeds and the grass growing wherever it feels like it. Pine needles and pine cones. All that underbrush. Roots crawling like snakes. Everything scattered all over the place. One big chaos. It's got to be put in order. Somebody ought to pick it all up, sort it out carefully, cut it down to size when necessary, and pack it all neatly in big boxes and little boxes. All that junk, all that crazy rubbish, it's got to be cleaned up.

That's cute, Gauthier. You certainly have ideas.

It's not cute and I haven't any ideas. It's just that I abominate all this disorder. Whichever way you look, all you see is a mess. That fir forest near Voroshenko wasn't a fir forest at all. That was only a manner of speaking. There were beeches, oaks, ash trees—all in a jumble.

But that's nature, Gauthier, it's beautiful.

You call it beautiful? I say it's horrible. You can't find your way. In the woods the trees are all mixed up, in the fields it's the poppies and buttercups. In the same thicket you find juniper, jasmine, and blackthorn. You call that beautiful? Anyway it's not for me. Everything topsy-turvy, like a, well, like a fair. It's enough to drive you mad. Pure madness.

Go on, with you everything's madness. It's nature, and nature is natural.

But not beautiful. There's nothing beautiful about it. A labyrinth. A blind alley. You can go in but you can't get out. And what's it like at night? Instead of two dozen stars there are billions, and they're so jumbled up you can't make head or tail of them. One and four is five, that's not so bad, I'm even willing to count to a thousand, but anything beyond that is no good. No, my dear Helga. It's awful.

But scientists know their way around.

I'm not a scientist. I'm a plain man. A plain man, it seems to me, also has a right to know where he is. But I'm lost. There's nothing to get your bearings by. But I'm going to let them cure me. That's what I'm going to do.

Did you really kill five people, Gauthier?

Yes. He turned to Helga. Yes, one and four.

For no reason?

I was ordered to.

And you worry your head about that? If you were ordered to, you're not responsible.

You don't think so?

Of course not.

I could also say I acted under hypnosis or that somebody got me drunk. I could say that. But there's something wrong. If a man like me lets himself be hypnotized, something's wrong. It proves that I'm sick. I've got to go to the hospital, I'm going tomorrow morning. I hope they still have my case record.

First you think your regiment is lost and now you're worried about your case record.

Yes, said Bachmann solemnly, that's the way I am. Something inside me is always looking for something. Like Faust. And Faust, Helga remembered from school, never found it, because he always wanted the wrong thing.

Isn't that tragic, Helga? That's tragic.

No, said Helga, it's dumb. What's lost is lost. Seek and ye shall find. You just have to look.

Helga, the worst of it isn't the five or the seven hundred and sixty-three. Those are numbers. What I lack is words. Haven't you ever noticed? I lack words. (He paused.) I'm afraid of the words I lack. When I left the house in Narvik, I had a vision and it's come true. I can still see it: a tree with dead branches, somebody's swinging an ax like mad, he chops off the branches, he fells the tree. He digs up the roots. Nothing's left, and the hole has hardly been filled in when a word grows up on the same spot—its name is tree—then he swallows the word . . . and dies. Words are poisonous. When you've got them in here (he indicated his stomach) they can make all kinds of trouble, but I keep them in my mouth, that's something else again, I speak them out right away and they're harmless. Isn't that clever? Talking is safer than dying. Isn't it? That's why I have to keep talking all the time. But I'm afraid it doesn't always work. People look at you so strangely. I'm always hunting for words. I can use them all. Big ones, little ones, thin ones, fat ones; even the weakest are better than nothing. . . .

And if you don't talk, you die! He raised his forefinger in warning: The dead are speechless, doesn't that prove it?

Talk away, said Helga sleepily.

She lay on the bed with closed eyes, she still had her coat on. She wasn't asleep, only benumbed by Bachmann's monotonous voice. Not only the police station and Muschel, but also Frau Gram, Bachmann, and the Brown Bear were a dream. Why do you have to talk? What's the good of it? she asked still more softly.

Bachmann had no desire to answer.

We have to call things by their names, he said. There's no use asking why. We just have to. Accurate descriptions. Things have to be right. If they're right in our mouths, everything's all right. Words must fit right. Got to dig them up. Wherever we can. You can find them any place if only you know how. They're under the stones, in the smallest things, in the most remote corners. Sometimes they crawl out of the ground, no bigger than little Schnotz. You only have to look. Or their name is scorpion or spider. That's two already. Ha ha. If you're smart, you can coax them out of the clouds. Isn't that wonderful? That gives us blue, atom, air, moon. There's something everywhere. You only have to know how to go about it. He was pleased with his disquisition. Helga whispered: why?

I can't explain any more. If she doesn't understand what I've told her, she won't understand anything. She is just dreaming. And what does a young girl dream about? Oh oh. Bachmann knew what the little things dream about. Love, passionate kisses. And the rest of it. (Even in his thoughts he wouldn't say the word.) The last time I put my foot in it. The last time I fell asleep. What can she think of me? He took the coat off and shook Helga awake. Get up, girl. Time to think of something else. Enough words. What we need now is a little romance. He removed his jacket and started on his shoes.

I've had trouble enough with romance. That's why she's throwing me out.

In that case, Helga, it's too late anyway. He took off his sweater. Where's the wash basin?

Next week I'll be out in the street. That doesn't seem to worry you.

Where's that basin? I've got to wash.

Helga took a large china basin with flowers on it out of the wash stand and poured water into it. Here's soap and a towel, but I think you'd better be going.

First Bachmann bared his torso, then (whistling through his teeth) unbuttoned his pants. In an instant he was stark naked.

Please don't, Helga said, it doesn't matter to you if I'm out in the street. Or I'll have to give her what she wants. What does she want? He sprinkled a few drops of water on his face, then he began, slowly and elaborately, to soap his private parts.

What she wants? You can imagine. For a year now I've refused. A week ago she gave me notice. Trying to blackmail me. She knows I can't stand the sight of myself.

You can't stand the sight of yourself? How so? Well, that's the main thing. The rest can wait. He dried himself. And now forward march, to bed. Before Helga could protest, Bachmann had drawn the sheet up to his chin. You can't stand the sight of yourself? That's interesting. Have you got a rash?

Of course not. Just this. She indicated her body, that's not a woman, tell me the honest truth, it's a whale. A whale? Bachmann was flabbergasted. Can she be a mind reader? Of course she's a fish, but the fish is all things. It's life, new beginning. Fertility. I'm a monster, Gauthier (she sat down beside him on the bed). Tell me sincerely.

Sincerely? Of course, I'm always sincere. I was only muddled. She clasped his shoulders in both hands and looked into his eyes: I beg of you, be frank with me. I can't stand lies. I'm an ugly monster.

Not at all, Helga, not at all.

Just tell me so, you don't have to pretend. No stupid compliments. I need the truth. I'm a whale, aren't I? Do you admit that I'm a whale? But Helga, you're not. . . . You're only . . . a little big.

Big? Yes, of course. Just tell me frankly to my face. Don't be a coward. I'm a whale, please tell me so.

Coward was too much for Bachmann: All right, if you insist. You're a whale, an ugly overgrown fish. You give me the creeps.

Helga was silent for a moment. She tried to smile but tears came instead: I knew it. She rested her head on his chest and sobbed. Now you've admitted it.

But Helga . . . I didn't mean it.

Not another word, she sobbed.

Bachmann sat up and stroked her hair. But Helga, that's not worth crying about. (He glanced at his nails to make sure they were clean.) People can't all be built the same way. I'm not exactly tiny myself.

She looked at him and tried to smile. Yes, that's a fact, she cried and laughed at once, you're not tiny either. Suddenly she was overcome with passion and cried: That's why we belong together, Gauthier, we were chosen. Fate picked us for each other.

She threw herself on him and kissed his shoulders, his chest and hands.

Calm down, Helga. Please calm down (she was biting his ear). Everything in proper order.

She stood up, undressed, and made for the bed.

No, no. Not like that. Wash first. Everything sweet and clean.

This man dominated her. I don't have to feel sorry for him. Maybe he's an exception. She washed herself. For a time they lay side by side, scarcely moving. Only the breathing of two pairs of lungs in the black darkness. Bachmann said something incomprehensible.

What's the matter? You're talking to yourself.

I've been thinking about Mirko Janko. You are the fairest woman on the continent. He played that marvelously. He's got a good voice too. You ought to be thinking about me, Helga pressed closer to him. I'm doing that too. You've got a fine voice too. Is that all? She pressed still closer.

Oh no. I like you.

Really?

Very much. I love you, Helga.

You love me?

Of course.

Yes, yes, of course. Then get started, honeybun, go ahead and love me.

Bachmann's right hand sprang into activity. His fingers wandered up and down. This is delightful. And so full of meaning. Every touch is a whole book of poems. How can I tell her that? I've got to say something or she'll think I'm all animal instinct, she'll think I'm like the rest of them. I wouldn't want that.

Your bosom is well shaped, Helga. The nipples are magnificent. How beautifully rounded the belly is. The pubic hair is as soft as silk. That's delightful. This little thing here is terrific, the way it reacts. The vagina is excellently proportioned, really splendid and not too little. The anus is fine too, the hair is short and woolly as it should be. The cheeks are a dream. Yes, I love you. Bachmann's voice sounded solemn and convincing.

Kiss me, Helga whispered passionately, why don't you kiss me? Actually, kissing struck him as unhygienic. Everyone knows that most infections are transmitted through the mouth. Besides it seemed too intimate. But this time he was willing to make an exception. He rolled over on Helga with all his weight and kissed her. For a few minutes he moved his tongue from left to right, feeling her palate and teeth with the tip. My, what sharp teeth she has!

For God's sake, Helga groaned, what are you waiting for?

Just a minute, girl. Just a minute. It's easier when the muscle's hard.

Does it take long, Gauthier?

Oh no, only half a second. There, there we are. Now, if you'll kindly . . . That's right. Thank you. Easy does it. Fine. And now. One, two, one . . .

You count so slowly.

One, two, one, two, one two, I can't go any faster. . . . Hm, there we are. Oh, it feels so good. Really splendid.

Darling, Helga whispered, darling. . . .

Bachmann moved back to his place and looked at the clock. Four hours, then I'll have to be going. He turned toward the wall, well, good night.

Good night, she turned her back to him. So this is what you let yourself in for! You're really crazy. Insane. Wanting to be dependent on a man. That's lunacy. He knows what he wants. He's not crazy. I am. She fell asleep.

The maid opens the door and at the far end of the vestibule Frau Doktor appears in a silk dress, smiling radiantly. Never mind, says Frau Doktor to the maid, the young lady has come to see me. The maid dissolves in the darkness. The consultation room is high class, full of paintings and statues. Red velvet. Chairs covered with gold-embroidered brocade. What luxury—

the rich have it soft. The white couch in the middle of the room doesn't fit in with the rest. Thick medical books on a desk in the window niche and beside it a small steel cabinet containing instruments. The polished chromium dazzles her. There's something I have to look up, says Frau Doktor, I won't be a second. Meanwhile make yourself comfortable. She helps her out of her coat and takes it out to the vestibule. She comes back smiling, sits down at the desk and leafs through a book.

She herself is sitting on the edge of a big, wide easy chair, staring at the hummingbirds and green bamboo bushes on the curtains. Her eyes keep turning back to the white couch. An operating table. It doesn't belong here. What am I doing here? I like this room, I wish I had one like it, it's so warm. Central heating. Compared to my wretched cold hovel—under the roof, frayed curtains. Why couldn't we swap? Frau Doktor stands up and invites her into the adjoining room. Shall we go in the drawing room and have a little talk, it's cozier. They pass through a double door. What a big room! Costly etchings and paintings, deep armchairs and an enormous bookcase full of old books. Warm light from standing lamps, the bay window is a garden full of plants and flowers. She feels poor and shabby and ashamed.

A bit of liqueur? You've had supper?

She nods and feels hungry. Frau Doktor picks up a crystal decanter and pours something that smells of sweet oranges. Frau Doktor sits facing her in an easy chair and says: My husband sends his apologies. A conference with the Führer.

Between the glasses on the low marble table, stands a single orchid in a long-stemmed vase. Lavender, brown and white. The orchid holds her spellbound.

A strange flower, says a voice, one would almost say an exotic animal. This is a special variety. A present from Hermann. It will soon be in full bloom. Look inside, she indicates the calyx, isn't it amazing? It's pink and red like raw meat. Orchids change their color, says the voice, but once they reach full bloom, they fade quickly. A rare, magnificent flower, no two are alike. But let's talk about you. What do you do? Oh yes, you're a teacher. You seem very independent. All alone in your little room. I lived that way as a student. Tell me about yourself. Say whatever comes into your head. But nothing comes into your head. She drains her liqueur. Instantly her glass is refilled. She drinks quickly. Frau Doktor smiles and pours again. Liqueur, warmth, and wealth. That's happiness. She tells the whole story of her life from the very beginning, but when she comes to Gauthier she stops. She won't mention him. She must guard his secret. In these surroundings his remark about the confusion and disorder of the German landscape might be misinterpreted. Gauthier is a member of the underground resistance, a careless word could mean court-martial.

But haven't you ever had a lover? A charming girl like you? Hasn't anybody ever told you how beautiful you are? No, nobody's told her, and if somebody did, it would be a lie. Then you're perfectly pure, like fresh-fallen snow? Frau Doktor smiles and the smile irritates her. After all she can't help it if she's big, but she won't admit to virgin. I've got a lover, she says, his name is Werner.

Do you see him often?

No, very seldom, he's at the front.

You young things, Frau Doktor takes a tone of maternal solicitude and reproach. We mustn't be old-fashioned in this day and age. If something has happened, he'll surely marry you. But you don't even know if you're fertile.

She blushes. Aren't you the silly little thing! And then Frau Doktor is sitting beside her, resting a fragrant hand on her shoulder. Why not consult a doctor? What are doctors for? The perfumed hand in her hair gives her an anguished feeling.

I'll have to take you under my wing, you have no parents here. Frau Doktor's mouth exhales rose perfume. Come, she says, and helps her up. All women aren't fertile, and only a doctor can tell.

Her will power is gone. She stands beside the white couch and wants to run away, but her legs refuse to carry her. Then suddenly she is lying on the table like a patient waiting to be examined. Maybe I really am sterile. That would be a disappointment for Gauthier. These aren't my office hours, says a voice, this is a service of friendship.

Her clothes are removed, she offers no resistance. A cushion is placed under her head. The room is overheated. A light, delicate hand is doing something on her thighs. Just a moment, she hears, just a moment, the examination is almost over.

Her body is burning, the perfume makes her head spin. She is under anesthetic. And now sideways, she hears through the mists, raise your knee to your chin. She obeys, something moves inside her, she trembles, clutches the table, but a hand takes her hand away, guides it. She touches something moist and warm. She is all in flames. She trembles. She falls. Her fingers look for support and reach deeper and more violently into the fiery furnace. Kisses rain down on her mouth and her breasts, they are a hot liquid that penetrates deep inside her. Gauthier, Gauthier, she tries to whisper, but she can't breathe. Her mouth is stifled and a moist soothing warmth carries her into a lake where she drowns.

Gauthier, Gauthier! Wake up . . . I've had a terrible dream. Gauthier. . . .

Bachmann woke up, saw that it was light outside, and immediately jumped out of bed. He dressed himself.

I had an awful dream, it was terrible. I drowned. With Frau Doktor Gram. It was terrible. I had a dream too, Bachmann said, dreaming is perfectly normal. Somebody swiped my bayonet, and when I try to take it away from him, he jumps at me and cuts my tongue out. I bled to death. I couldn't talk.

She made me lie down on a white bed, Gauthier, and then she . . .

And when I died, Bachmann interrupted, the same man comes along, he sees I'm dead, and says: Come on, man, get moving—they're waiting for you. Don't be a slacker—when I was already dead.

And she said, Helga remembered, that maybe I was sterile. You should have seen the room—those bare empty walls, all black. But I can feel the fire. It's burning somewhere inside me. Everything's gray, but the fire's not all out.

Smoke sometimes comes out of my mouth too, said Bachmann. I often have burning inside me. Maybe both of us are burning and haven't noticed it. But now I have to go. Be good, Helga.

Just don't make any noise on the stairs—step softly—so she doesn't catch you. Carry your shoes. Bachmann was already outside, he stuck his head through the door: I'm going to the hospital, Helga. The treatment may take a while, weeks, maybe months. When I'm well again, I'll come back.

Where are you going?

To the hospital to be cured. I'm very sick.

Helga propped herself on her right elbow and looked him over. He wasn't making faces, he wasn't twitching, he didn't look idiotic. You couldn't tell by his face. You don't look it, said Helga (he's unfair to himself, poor man). She felt sorry for him.

I know, Bachmann whispered, it doesn't show.

Just a second, Gauthier (Gauthier had a look of impatience), what's your sickness called? Is it contagious?

Bachmann shrugged his shoulders: I don't know. But now I have to go.

He closed the door carefully before Helga had a chance to tell him that Frau Doktor Gram would be sure to support his appeal.

THE DIAGNOSIS WAS NOT DIVULGED, the cure only took ten minutes. When his turn finally came (the whole German Army seemed to have assembled in the Honnef hospital), he modestly bowed his head, looked at his cap which he held in his hand, and whispered: I accept the decision of the medical commission and withdraw my appeal. I am perfectly willing to be discharged as soon as possible, but request further treatment.

Your name? an orderly inquired.

Gauthier Bachmann.

The orderly went to a filing cabinet, leafed through the letter B for a few minutes, mumbling Ba, Ba, Ba—and came back with a card. Gauthier Bachmann, born in Duisburg May 15, 1919.

That's right, said Bachmann.

The orderly laid the card on the table.

Dr. Wieland Perm, a pipesmoker in his fifties with a round red face, first assistant in the neurology section, sucked at his pipe, looked from the card to Bachmann and back to the card, and read: December 11, 1943, Sergeant Gauthier Bachmann has been examined. State of health: excellent. He is fit for service and is to be returned to his unit at once. Request for discharge submitted by Medical Corps Major T. Werner and Medical Corps Captain H. E. Bückel is hereby rejected.

That must be a mistake, Doctor, it's impossible. Dr. Perm blew out smoke, took his pipe out of his mouth and said: I repeat, and he repeated the entry on the card word for word.

You're perfectly healthy, my boy, as officially attested on December 11, 1943.

178

What's that again? Bachmann looked in bewilderment from the doctor to the orderly.

My dear man, you can't expect me to read it again, here it is in black and white. If you'd like to see for yourself, go ahead. Bachmann picked up his card with trembling hand and read aloud. December 11, 1943. Sergeant Gauthier Bachmann, that's me, has been examined. State of health: Excellent. He put the card down.

What's wrong with you? Does my pipe bother you?

Me? I? Nothing . . . Bachmann stuttered.

Are you on home leave or what?

Me? No. I'm not here at all. I don't exist. He clutched his head. I don't understand. No, it's impossible. You're telling me I'm in good health?

Your health is perfect. Dismissed from hospital on December 11. Complete recovery.

Recovery?

Are you deaf?

No, not in the least.

Orderly, give the man a chair, he's wobbling. He sat down with a sigh. I went over the hill in 1943 because, well, I was afraid they were going to discharge me.

Yes, a request was put in, but they turned it down.

Somebody, I don't remember who it was, said: Bachmann, I hear you're up for a discharge. So I went over the hill.

And where have you been keeping yourself?

All over. From Palermo to Narvik. I, I've been looking for my regiment. I swear I was looking for my regiment.

But you went in the wrong direction. Your regiment's on the eastern front.

But it was almost wiped out and then they patched it up again. That's what somebody told me, because a regiment can't just vanish off the face of the earth, can it, and my being alive doesn't prove a damn thing.

A healthy young man, Sergeant Bachmann, in the prime of life, with your build, barely twenty-five and you just shove off, leaving your comrades in the lurch.

But, but . . . I'm not dreaming?

You don't look it. Man, you're in perfect health. It says so right here. We'll do our demobilizing after the war, right now there's a war on. Germany needs every man. Bachmann stood up and went like a sleepwalker to the door. Are you sure? Doctor, sir, are you sure I'm in good health?

Get a move on, man! You're not my only patient. As far as we're concerned, you're in good health and fit for service. Your imagination is no business of ours.

Doctor, sir, Bachmann turned his right foot in, he wasn't prepared to go yet, one more thing. Suppose some Xaver Schnotz promises you white kitchens when you're nearly starved and Mürz, the master sergeant, double-crosses you, I mean, suppose all your plans go up in smoke like the tobacco in your pipe even if you do get the liver, well, I mean, then . . . You'll shoot anybody that's tied, won't you?

Let's not exaggerate, Sergeant, let's not exaggerate. You're deceiving yourself.

Oh no, Bachmann argued, pleased that the doctor had listened to him. I'm not deceiving myself. When a major and a lieutenant conspire against a subordinate and try to ruin him, and then somebody comes along and talks about courage and humanity, what else can you do? You've got to go along. Because one fine day the armor plate bursts, doesn't it? What do you know about armor plate, you infantryman? the doctor interrupted. It's got to burst, Bachmann repeated passionately, and if you don't shoot holes in it with bullets and hammer on it with your fists, if you take it lying down like some people, where will you be? How are you going to get through?

What are you driving at, Sergeant?

How are you going to get through, said Bachmann, that's all I want to know. You do it or it's done to you. You know what I mean. . . .

That's enough, Dr. Perm shouted, threatening him with his pipe as if it were a revolver, all you can think about is obscenities. Close the door. Bachmann, who was holding the handle, closed the door.

You're perfectly right, said Dr. Perm in a loud whisper, and because he was in agreement with his superior, the orderly looked discreetly at his fingernails and began biting his thumbnail.

You're right, you're a man of intelligence and feeling. But that only proves the examiners were right. You're perfectly healthy, healthier than a good many people. You don't know it yet, but never mind, you will some day. You're as normal as anybody can be. But you're a malingerer. Am I right, Fritz? The orderly spat a piece of nail out elegantly and said: Of course you're right, Wieland. He's normal, just look at the way he's standing. As soon as he hears the word, he starts up, it's typical. Bachmann's hands and feet had turned sharply inward, giving him the air of helplessness which lends charm to a man of Bachmann's dimensions.

That's quite a guy, Fritz, what do you think?

He's no trained seal, Wieland.

He's got something, don't you think?

It's with men like him that history's made, Wieland. Fritz bit the nail of his little finger.

Wouldn't you say he was slightly perverse, Fritz?

Not at all. No more than the rest of us.

You wouldn't call him a victim of Germany's war for survival?

Nonsense, Wieland. He's above considerations of nationality. He lives in wartime and when peace comes, he doesn't die. He can be used for anything, there's nothing he's not capable of. The salt of the earth.

An overdose is fatal, Fritz.

Not to the salt, Wieland, only to people.

Forward march! Back to your unit, Sergeant Bachmann.

Meanwhile Bachmann had let his head hang down and was craning his neck in an effort to look up at the ceiling. He pressed his arms to his sides, but his fingers were flabby and lifeless. He saw nothing and didn't hear a word of what they were saying about him. Only the word MARCH shook him out of his half sleep. Dr. Perm called after him: The death penalty is still in force for desertion. Just a friendly hint.

IN THE GRASS BY THE RIVER BANK he opened his coat and tunic, pushed up his sweater and undid two shirt buttons. He wanted to feel his heart with his fingers. The heat of the day lay heavy, like too much tenderness, over the gray and green colors of the Rhine. The ticking he heard was the engine of a barge. Then with wide-open eyes he saw more barges floating through the mist that rose from the water. They're carrying fuel to hell and stones for the wall of the city of the dead. Desertion leads to a quarry. Branches growing out of the clouds. Schnotz says: Your turn will come. What's written on the barges? Basel, Rotterdam. Aha! Secret names of the gates to the other world. Cement, stones, sand. A giant is carrying them through the water on his shoulders, wading step by step through the mud. A fool. Who told him to do that? If he'd pick up the cargo and throw it all overboard, and if the other giants did the same, we'd all be saved. The chunks of red meat would be cleared away. The crime can be discovered any day. What then? Upstream and downstream they go, day after day like galley slaves, they would have the power to sweep away the danger. Only the giants are strong enough. I'm one of them. When it is all put under the concrete and the sun shines fiercely on it, nobody'll know any more what's underneath. The corpus delicti will be gone. Nothing is more dangerous than sitting still. I'm shoving off.

Bachmann stood up. A few feet away, a little higher up on the bank, a schoolboy was lying in the grass. He seemed to be about ten years old. His school satchel lay beside him. He looked disheveled and hungry as if he had been playing hooky for a week and roaming around in the fields to avoid going home. He had been looking down at Bachmann the whole time, impressed by his size. It intrigued him to see the soldier undoing his clothes to put his hand on his chest. You're awfully big, he said admiringly.

What's your name? Bachmann asked.

Walter.

Air-raid warning, Walter suddenly shouted. It could be heard very softly in the distance. Just as suddenly the sirens of Honnef began to howl, so loud and shrill that both took fright. Walter looked up. His little thin face grew sharp, he listened with his eyes. At least two thousand of them. They're heading this way.

How do you know?

I can tell.

The sirens continued to howl without interruption like a chorus of wailing women. Electrical sighs mourned the destruction of thousands of little machines that were still in working order. Coming? Bachmann asked. Walter ran up the embankment and attached himself to Bachmann.

We've got to get Helga, said Bachmann. Let's go, maybe she's still asleep.

Walter was too confused to say anything. He was proud that this big soldier had taken him in tow. Everywhere people were craning their necks like prisoners pressing their heads through the bars to breathe the fresh air of freedom before the guard's shrill whistle should call them back.

HELGA WAS SHAKEN roughly awake. The giant, somebody screamed, it's disgraceful. Who do you think you are?

What? Helga asked sleepily. Giant? You're seeing ghosts.

Frau Gram was standing over her. Don't you dare to speak to me like that!

It's still my room until I move.

Which is right away, this minute. Muschel phoned. There's a giant sleeping under your roof, he says. He didn't have to tell me, I saw him leaving. You always see them leaving. Ghosts is what you see. And now I want to sleep. Don't bother me.

The tone was new to Frau Gram. The ungrateful creature, she's going too far. Her friends were right. You'll live to regret your generosity. Not taking money for the room is stupid enough. And what are they saying now? You've taken a serpent to your bosom, throw her out, Else, before it's too late.

Helga, I've had enough. Get up and pack your things. Immediately.

I want to sleep, Helga turned over on the other side. You can sleep at the police station. This is my house, my room, and you're sleeping in my bed. Get out, I say. She pulled at the blanket, but Helga held it fast. It's my pillow and my blankets. Are you going to get up or not?

I want to sleep, Helga screamed.

Not in my bed. With one tug she had the sheet and blankets off. Helga was naked and cold, and so angry the words couldn't come. They stuck in her throat and almost choked her. In your bed! Yes, in your bed, she shouted in a sudden frenzy. In your bed, I've been lying in your bed since the first day, you fiend!

185

She leaped wildly through the room with flying hair. Frau Doktor Gram went ashen pale. Service of friendship! Helga fumed at her. Some friendship! You damned whore! Laying hands on a minor. You, you pervert! Picking orchids, eh, that's your style! Haven't you got a lover? Helga mimicked her voice. It's none of your God-damn business whether I have a lover. And besides I'm pregnant. She thumped her belly. It's all in here. The whole lot. Giants, midgets, monkeys with one leg, with four legs. Not like you, she slapped Frau Gram's belly with the back of her hand. It's empty, there's life in mine. Dancing and bubbling and boiling. You've got a pig's bladder, not a womb. Come here—I'll give you one of mine. Three heads shorter, weak and transfixed with fear, Frau Gram stood unresisting as Helga ripped her clothes off. Helga threw her on the bed, kneaded her with both hands, and rode her like an Amazon riding an exhausted horse: I'm the giant, Helga screamed, I'm the giant. You've got it coming to you! Then she squeezed her neck until a little slow stream flowed from her lips. As soon as Helga saw the blood, she let go, jumped up, threw a few articles of clothing into a bag and ran down the stairs. In the house door stood Bachmann, a big sinister shadow.

Where are you going? Bachmann asked. There's an air raid, you can't go out.

I've got to see Muschel, Helga bellowed. I've got to wring his neck.

You're not going anywhere, Bachmann held both her wrists and closed the door with his foot.

Who's that? Helga had seen Walter, who was standing in a dark corner of the hallway, overwhelmed by the sight of the naked woman.

It's Walter. I found him down by the river. He's playing hooky. Where's the cellar? There's going to be fireworks in a minute.

That's the way to the air-raid shelter, came Walter's voice. He pointed at an arrow. Helga struggled: Let me go, let me go. No, said Bachmann firmly, picked her up and carried her down the hallway like a father carrying his sick child. Walter went ahead. Just as they reached the entrance to the dark shaft, the ground trembled. The earth seemed to open and pulled them downward, hugging them more and more violently, to smother them in her embrace.

THE TREMOR HAD DIED AWAY, the vibration stopped, but deep down where life begins there was movement, bowels burst and lungs exploded, internal organs fell open like oranges. Eyesockets were full of worms that fed on meat and ears were hosts to gnawing vermin.

Tongues dangled dead, strings that had snapped apart, fingernails broken in the wet ground. Their joints had come undone, their teeth lay loose in their mouths. Not mummified but old as time, they lay in their overcoats and stared upward. It was pitchdark, the lamp had used up the last remaining oxygen. Somewhere, scarcely audible, water flowed from a burst pipe. The water murmured, trickled and dripped, spoke slowly and suddenly screamed: Get up, children, it's time.

No god could have spoken a more solemn command. They stood up. First Bachmann, then Helga, and groped their way through the darkness to the ladder. As if they had just awakened from a stupor, they climbed slowly and wearily rung by rung. They rose from the grave to the surface of the earth and looked around. As far as the eye could see a desert of ashes under a lead-gray sky. The stillness was palpable, as colorless and bare as the walls of a monk's cell. Nothing moved in the deathly silence, nothing crawled, rustled, or murmured. Only the breathing of those two—little Walter had vanished. Bachmann had a pleasant, familiar feeling of well-being, like a memory that lay far behind. He recognized something and couldn't yet believe it. We're in Paradise, Helga, his voice had no echo. Helga, too, felt something that she remembered from early childhood. Or was it still further back?

The gray ocean of an extinguished landscape made them feel strangely happy. Everything fitted strangely together.

Yes, this must be Paradise, she said, and couldn't quite believe that such a thing could be experienced.

It's unbelievable, Gauthier, we'll have to get used to it. Bachmann said nothing. His chest rose and fell. Breathing was more important to him than talking.

Where's the boy? Helga asked.

Little Walter? Oh, Bachmann motioned with his hand, he must be up ahead or maybe he's still down below. But not alive. Come, Helga, we've got to be going, we can't stay here.

For six hours they marched, grim and silent, without a halt, and by nightfall they came to a small crop of trees and water. They hadn't met a soul all day, only once Bachmann thought he saw a dog, running through the bare countryside, whimpering and barking. (But maybe it was a delusion.) The water was a little pond, hardly more than a pool of rain water and just as muddy. They cleared the ashes, charred wood, and burned leaves from a few square feet of ground, spread out the overcoat and lay down.

That first night in their Paradise they were afraid like helpless little children. They hid with their faces to the ground though no one was looking for them, and hardly dared to breathe though no one was listening. They heard branches falling and animals crawling through the thicket, but there were no branches or animals. The stones they heard falling into the water might just as well have been the old illusions bursting with a slight pop. Out of Helga's mouth grew blood-red flowers, which blossomed in an eddy of words.

Bright infant's eyes glittering green in the blue grass. Flaming red cheeks in the hot ashes. The sun hovers red and flat in the sky, unwilling either to rise or to set. All things have changed their face, the seed is ripe, the eyes are falling from the trees. We must gather them up.

When her mouth closed like a scar, Bachmann said, speaking through her throat: What infant's eyes? What seed? You're delirious. You're sick.

Her throat quivered like a snake. With his forehead he nuzzled her jugular vein, it felt like a backbone. Her nostrils were narrow and dark like little holes in the ground where worms disappear at night. Her cheeks were as white as kneaded dough. He closed his eyes and threw his left leg and left arm over her. Like creepers on a giant tree in the virgin forest they sank deep into the bark. Behind closed eyelids he saw the brown Cyclopses of her breasts, he slid over the bloated white body, grazed the reddish weeds that grew out of the hollow, and dwelt at length on the fattened turkey backs of her haunches. Like an enormous white whale on dry land, his prey quaked beneath him. He was at the end of his strength. Why had he pulled the dying beast out of the ocean? To let it rot in the heat. Everything about it was contaminated. And he had tasted of it. His stomach tightened like a clam, fought off a deadly spasm. The sweetish taste of pestilence was painful to his palate. The plague had fought its way into his brain cells. He felt millions of tiny crabs clinging to an abscess. Too late for help, nothing that can be done, remedy is nothing but a word, stale medicine, nothing can revive dead cells. But I hauled her ashore. Risked a life to lose a life. The madness of his act crashed down on him like a giant wave. Water rushed into his lungs as if they were empty hoses, he couldn't breathe. He bared his long yellow teeth, buried his nose still deeper in her neck and bit into her throat.

Then he stood up and marched off toward the East, toward the war, to search for his regiment once more.

Jakov Lind (1926-2007) was born Heinz Jakov Landwirth in Vienna in 1927 to an assimilated Jewish family. Arriving in the Netherlands as a part of the Kindertransport in 1939, Lind survived the Second World War by fleeing into Germany, where he disguised himself as a Dutch deckhand on a barge on the Rhine. Following the war, he spent several years in Israel and Vienna before finally settling in London in 1954. It was in London that he wrote, first in German and later in English, the novels, short stories, and autobiographies that made his reputation, including his masterpieces: *Landscape in Concrete*, *Ergo*, and *Soul of Wood*. Regarded in his lifetime as a successor to Beckett and Kafka, Lind was posthumously awarded the Theodor Kramer Prize in 2007.

Ralph Manheim (1907–1992) was one of the great translators of the twentieth Century. He translated the works of Günter Grass, Bertolt Brecht, Louis-Ferdinand Céline, Hermann Hesse, Peter Handke, Novalis, and Martin Heidegger, among many others. In 1982, PEN American Center created an award—the Ralph Manheim Medal for Translation—in his name, which honors a translator whose career has demonstrated a commitment to excellence through the body of his or her work.

Open Letter—the University of Rochester's nonprofit, literary translation press—is one of only a handful of publishing houses dedicated to increasing access to world literature for English readers. Publishing twelve titles in translation each year, Open Letter searches for works that are extraordinary and influential, works that we hope will become the classics of tomorrow.

Making world literature available in English is crucial to opening our cultural borders, and its availability plays a vital role in maintaining a healthy and vibrant book culture. Open Letter strives to cultivate an audience for these works by helping readers discover imaginative, stunning works of fiction and by creating a constellation of international writing that is engaging, stimulating, and enduring.

Current and forthcoming titles from Open Letter include works from Argentina, Austria, Brazil, France, Iceland, Lithuania, Spain, and numerous other countries.

www.openletterbooks.org